P9-AFH-887

Ronia,
The Robber's Daughter

OTHER BOOKS BY ASTRID LINDGREN

Pippi Longstocking
Pippi Goes on Board
Pippi in the South Seas
Pippi on the Run
The Brothers Lionheart
The Children of Noisy Village
Christmas in Noisy Village

ASTRID LINDGREN

RONIA, The Robber's Daughter

TRANSLATED BY
PATRICIA CROMPTON

The Viking Press, New York

First American Edition

Originally published in 1981 as RONJA RÖVARDOTTER by Rabén & Sjögren Bokforlag, Stockholm.
Published in 1983 by The Viking Press
40 West 23rd Street, New York, N.Y. 10010
Published simultaneously in Canada by
Penguin Books Canada Limited
Printed in U.S.A.
1 2 3 4 5 87 86 85 84 83

Library of Congress Cataloging in Publication Data
Lindgren, Astrid, date Ronia, the robber's daughter.
Translation of: Ronja rövardotter.
Summary: Ronia, who lives with her father and his band of robbers in a castle in the woods, causes trouble when she befriends the son of a rival robber chieftain.
1. Robbers and outlaws—Fiction I. Title.
PZ7.L6585Ro 1983 [Fic] 82-60081 ISBN 0-670-60640-5

Ronia,
The Robber's Daughter

One

On the night that Ronia was born a thunderstorm was raging over the mountains, such a storm that all the goblinfolk in Matt's Forest crept back in terror to their holes and hiding places. Only the fierce harpies preferred stormy weather to any other and flew, shrieking and hooting, around the robbers' stronghold on Matt's mountain. Their noise disturbed Lovis, who was lying within, preparing to give birth, and she said to Matt, "Drive the hell-harpies away and let me have some quiet. Otherwise I can't hear what I'm singing!"

The fact was that Lovis liked to sing while she was having her baby. It made things easier, she insisted, and the baby would probably be all the jollier if it arrived on earth to the sound of a song.

Matt took his crossbow and shot off a few arrows through one of the arrow slits of the fort. "Be off with you, harpies!" he shouted. "I'm going to have a baby tonight—get that into your heads, you hags!"

"Ho, ho, he's going to have a baby tonight," hooted the harpies. "A thunder-and-lightning baby, small and ugly it'll be, ho, ho!"

Then Matt shot again, straight into the flock, but they simply jeered at him and flew off across the treetops, hooting angrily.

While Lovis lay there, giving birth and singing, and while Matt quelled the wild harpies as best he could, his robbers were sitting by the fire down in the great stone hall, eating and drinking and behaving as rowdily as the harpies themselves. After all, they had to do something while they waited, and all twelve of them were waiting for what was about to happen up there in the tower room. No child had ever been born in Matt's Fort in all their robber days there.

Noddle-Pete was waiting most of all.

"That robber baby had better come soon," he said. "I'm old and rickety, and my robbing days will soon be over. It would be fine to see a new robber chief here before I'm finished."

He had scarcely stopped speaking when the door opened and Matt rushed in, quite witless with delight. He raced all the way around the hall, leaping high with joy and shrieking like a madman.

"I've got a child! Do you hear me—I've got a child!"

"What sort of child is it?" asked Noddle-Pete over in his corner.

"A robber's daughter, joy and gladness!" shouted Matt. "A robber's daughter—here she comes!"

And over the high threshold stepped Lovis with her baby in her arms. All the robbers' noise turned off at once.

"I do believe that's made your beer go down the wrong way," said Matt. He took the baby girl from Lovis and carried her around among the robbers.

"Here! Want to see the most beautiful child ever born in a robbers' fort?"

His daughter lay there in his arms, looking up at him with wide, bright eyes.

"That child understands just about everything already—you can see that," said Matt.

"What will you call her?" asked Noddle-Pete.

"Ronia," said Lovis. "I decided that a long time ago."

"What if it had been a boy?" said Noddle-Pete.

Lovis gave him a calm, stern look. "If I decide my baby is to be called Ronia, it will *be* a Ronia!"

Then she turned to Matt. "Shall I take her now?"

But Matt did not want to hand over his daughter. He stood there gazing in admiration at her clear eyes, her little mouth, her black tufts of hair, her helpless hands, and he trembled with love.

"You, baby, you're already holding my robber heart in those little hands," he said. "I don't understand it, but that's how it is."

"Could I hold her for a bit?" Noddle-Pete asked, and Matt laid Ronia in his arms as if she were a golden egg.

"I give you the new robber chieftain you've been talking about all this time. Don't drop her, whatever you do, or it will be your last hour!"

But Noddle-Pete just smiled his toothless smile at Ronia. "There's no real weight to her," he said, surprised, raising and lowering her a couple of times.

That made Matt angry, and he snatched his baby back. "What did you expect, numskull? A great fat robber chieftain with a bulging belly and a pointed beard, eh?"

All the robbers realized then that there must be no comments about this child if they wanted to keep Matt in a good mood. And it really was not wise to annoy him. So they set to work at once, praising and extolling the newborn baby. They also emptied a great many tankards of beer in her honor, which made Matt happy. He threw himself down on his high seat among them and showed off his remarkable child again and again.

"This is going to plague the life out of Borka," said Matt. "He can sit there in his miserable robbers' den and gnash his teeth with jealousy. Yes, death and destruction! There will be such a gnashing that all the wild harpies and gray dwarfs in Borka's Wood will hold their ears, believe me!"

Noddle-Pete nodded gleefully and said with a little snigger, "Sure enough, it will plague the life out of Borka. Now Matt's line will live on, but Borka's line will be finished and done for."

"Yes," said Matt, "finished and done for, sure as death! As far as I know, Borka has not managed to get a child, and is not likely to either."

Then came a crack of thunder the like of which had never been heard in Matt's Wood before. It made even the robbers turn pale, and Noddle-Pete fell flat on his back, weak as he was. A piteous little cry came unexpectedly from Ronia, and that shook Matt worse than the thunderclap.

"My child's crying!" he shrieked. "What do we do, what do we do?"

But Lovis was standing by calmly. She took the baby from him and put her to her breast, and there was no more crying.

"That was a good crack," said Noddle-Pete, when he too had calmed down a little. "I'll take my dying oath it struck."

Yes, the lightning had struck and in earnest, too, as they saw when morning came. The ancient fortress high up on Matt's Mountain had been cleft down the middle. From the highest battlements to the deepest vault of the dungeons, the fortress was now split in two halves, with a chasm between them.

"Ronia, your young life has gotten off to a grand start," said Lovis, as she stood by the shattered wall with the baby in her arms, looking at the disaster.

Matt was raging like a wild animal. How could this have been allowed to happen to his forefathers' old fortress? But Matt could not go on being angry about anything for long, and he could always find reasons to take comfort.

"Oh, well, we shan't have so many twists and turns and cellar pits and rubbish to keep track of. And perhaps no one will need to get lost in Matt's Fort any more. Remember what it was like when Noddle-Pete went astray and didn't turn up for four days!"

Noddle-Pete did not enjoy being reminded of this occasion. Was it his fault he had gotten lost? He had only been trying to find out how vast and rambling Matt's Fort really was, and had indeed found it big enough to get lost in. Poor thing, he was almost half dead before he finally found his way back to the great stone hall. Thank goodness the robbers had been bawling and kicking up enough noise for him to hear them a long way off; otherwise he would never have gotten back.

"In any case, we have never used the whole fort," said Matt, "and we will go on living in our hall and bedrooms and tower rooms where we have always lived. The only thing that annoys me is that we have lost our outhouse. Yes, death and destruction! It's on the other side of the chasm now, and I'm sorry for anyone who can't contain himself until we manage to build a new one."

But that was soon dealt with, and life in Matt's Fort went on exactly as before—except that now there was a child there. A little child, who succeeded bit by bit in sending Matt and all his robbers more or less mad, in Lovis's view. Not that it hurt them to become a little gentler-handed and milder-mannered, but there should be moderation in all things. And it really was strange to see twelve robbers and one robber chieftain sitting there like a lot of sheep, beaming and blissful just because a small child had learned to crawl around the stone hall, as if there had never been a greater miracle on earth. It was true that Ronia scampered about unusually fast because she had a trick of pushing off with her left foot, which the robbers thought absolutely astounding. But, after all, most children do learn to crawl, as Lovis said, *without* loud cheers, and without their father seeing it as a reason to forget everything else and positively neglect his work.

"Do you want Borka to take over all the robbing in Matt's Forest as well?" she asked sharply, when the robbers, with Matt at their head, came storming home early just because they had to see Ronia eating her porridge before Lovis put her into her hanging cradle for the night.

But Matt had no ears for such talk.

"Ronia mine, my little pigeon," he shouted, as Ronia, shoving hard with her left foot, came shooting across the floor toward him as soon as he walked in the door. And he sat with his little pigeon on his knee and fed her her porridge while his twelve robbers looked on. The porridge bowl was standing on the hearth at arm's reach, and as Matt was rather clumsy with his rough robber's fists, a lot of porridge got spilled on the floor, and Ronia knocked the spoon from time to time, so that a good deal of porridge also flew onto Matt's eyebrows. The first time it happened, the robbers laughed so uproariously that Ronia was frightened and began to cry, but she soon realized that she had hit on something amusing to do, and did it again, which delighted the robbers more than it amused Matt. But otherwise Matt thought that everything Ronia did was incomparable and that she herself had not her equal on earth.

Even Lovis had to laugh when she saw Matt sitting there with his child on his knee and porridge on his eyebrows.

"My dear Matt, who would ever think that you were the most powerful robber chieftain in all the woods and mountains! If Borka saw you now, he would split his sides laughing."

"I'd soon put a stop to that," Matt said calmly.

Borka—Borka was the archenemy. Just as Borka's father and grandfather had been the archenemies of Matt's father and grandfather—yes, since time immemorial the Borkas and the Matts had been at loggerheads. They had always been robbers and a terror to decent folk who had to pass with their horses and wagons through the deep forests where the robbers lurked.

"God help anyone whose way lies along Robbers' Walk," people said, talking of the narrow mountain pass between Borka's Wood and Matt's Wood. There were always robbers on the lookout there, and whether they were Borka's robbers or Matt's robbers made little difference, at least to those who were robbed. But to Matt and Borka the difference was enormous. They fought for their lives over the booty and even robbed each other without hesitation if there were not enough merchants passing through Robbers' Walk.

Ronia knew nothing of all this; she was too young. She did not know that her father was a feared robber chieftain. To her, he was just the kind, bearded Matt, who laughed and sang and shouted and gave her porridge, and whom she loved.

But she was growing up every day, and soon she began to explore the world around her. For a long time she had believed that the great stone hall was the whole world. And she liked it there; she was safe sitting under the great long table, playing with pebbles and pinecones that Matt brought home to her. And the stone hall was not a bad place for a child. You could have great fun there, and you could learn a lot.

Ronia liked it when the robbers sang around the fire in the evenings. She sat quietly under the table, listening, until she knew all the robbers' ditties by heart. Then she joined in, her voice clear as a bell, and Matt was astonished at his matchless child, who sang so well. She taught herself to dance, too. If the robbers were in the mood, they would dance and leap around the room like madmen, and Ronia soon saw what to do. She danced and bounded and made robber leaps as well, to Matt's delight, and when afterward the robbers threw themselves down at the long table to slake their thirst with a tankard of beer, he bragged about his daughter.

"She's as beautiful as a wild harpy, I'd have you know! As supple, as dark-eyed, and as black-haired. You never saw such a splendid child in your lives, I'd have you know!"

And the robbers nodded and agreed with him. But Ronia sat silently under the table with her pebbles and pinecones, and when she saw the robbers' feet in their shaggy fur slippers, she pretended that they were her unruly goats. She had seen some in the goat shed, where Lovis took her when she did the milking.

But Ronia had seen little more than this during her short life. She knew nothing of what lay outside Matt's Fort. And one fine day Matt realized—however little he liked it—that the time had come.

"Lovis," he said to his wife, "our child must learn what it's like living in Matt's Forest. Let her go!"

"Ah, so you've seen it at last," said Lovis. "It would have happened long ago if I'd had my way."

And from then on Ronia was free to wander at will. But first Matt had one or two things to say to her.

"Watch out for wild harpies and gray dwarfs and Borka robbers," he said.

"How will I know which are wild harpies and gray dwarfs and Borka robbers?" asked Ronia.

"You'll find out," Matt said.

"All right," said Ronia.

"And watch out you don't get lost in the forest," said Matt.

"What shall I do if I get lost in the forest?" Ronia asked.

"Find the right path," Matt said.

"All right," said Ronia.

"And watch out you don't fall in the river," Matt said.

"What shall I do if I fall in the river?" Ronia asked.

"Swim," Matt said.

"All right," said Ronia.

"And watch out you don't tumble into Hell's Gap," Matt said. He meant the chasm that split Matt's Fort in two.

"What shall I do if I tumble into Hell's Gap?" Ronia asked.

"You won't be doing anything else," Matt said, and then he gave a bellow, as if all things evil had suddenly pierced his heart.

"All right," said Ronia when Matt had finished bellowing. "I shan't fall into Hell's Gap. Is there anything else?"

"There certainly is," said Matt. "But you'll find out bit by bit. Go now!"

Two

So RONIA WENT. SHE SOON REALIZED HOW STUPID SHE HAD BEEN: how could she have thought that the great stone hall was the whole world? Not even the huge Matt's Fort was the whole world. Not even the high Matt's Mountain was the whole world—no, the world was bigger than Matt. It was so big that it took your breath away. Of course, she had heard Matt and Lovis talking about things beyond Matt's Fort; they had talked of the river. But it was not until she could see how it came rushing in wild rapids from deep under Matt's Mountain that she understood what rivers were. They had talked about the forest. But it was not until she saw it, so dark and mysterious, with all its rustling trees, that she understood what forests were, and she laughed silently because rivers and forests were there. She could scarcely believe it.

She followed the path straight into the wildest woods and came to the lake. Matt had told her that she must not go farther than that. And the lake lay there, black among the dark pines. Only the water lilies floating on its surface gleamed white. Ronia did not know that they were water lilies, but she looked at them for a long time and laughed silently because water lilies were there.

She stayed by the lake all day and did many things there that she had never tried before. She threw pinecones into the water and tried to see if she could make them bob away just by splashing with her feet. She had never had such fun before. Her feet felt so glad and free when she made them splash, and gladder still when she made them climb. There were great mossy boulders around the pool to climb on, and pine trees and fir trees to clamber in. Ronia climbed and clambered until the sun began to sink behind the wooded ridges. Then she ate the bread and drank the milk she had brought with her. She lay down on the moss to rest for a while, and the trees rustled high above her head. She lay there watching them and laughed silently because they were there. Then she fell asleep.

When she woke up, the evening had grown dark and she could see the stars burning above the treetops. Then she realized that there was even more to the world than she had thought. And it made her sad that stars were there but she could never reach them, no matter how far she stretched her arms toward them.

Now she had been in the forest longer than she was allowed. Now she must go home; otherwise, she knew, Matt would be out of his mind.

The stars were mirrored in the lake; everything else was deepest darkness. But she was used to darkness; it did not frighten her. How dark it was in Matt's Fort on winter nights, when the fire had gone out—darker than any wood. No, she was not afraid of darkness.

Just as she was ready to go, she remembered the leather bag she had brought her food in. The bag was still up on the boulder where she had sat to eat, so she climbed up in the darkness to get it. She had the idea that here on the high boulder she was closer to the stars, and she stretched up her hands to see if she could pick some to take home with her in the leather bag. But it was no use, so she took her bag and began to climb down.

Then she saw something that frightened her. Everywhere, among the trees, eyes were gleaming. There was a ring of eyes all around the stone, watching her, and she had not noticed anything. Never before had she seen eyes that shone in the darkness, and she did not like them.

"What do you want?" she cried, but got no answer. Instead the eyes came closer. Slowly, a little bit at a time, they drew nearer and nearer, and she could hear a murmur of voices, strange, gray old voices muttering and droning all together.

"Gray dwarfs all! Human here, human here in gray dwarfs' wood! Gray dwarfs all, bite and strike, gray dwarfs all, bite and strike!"

And suddenly they were right below the stone, extraordinary gray creatures which wished her ill. She could not see them, but she knew they were there, and it made her shudder. Now she knew how dangerous they were, the gray dwarfs Matt had told her to look out for. But it was too late now.

For now they were beginning to beat on the stone with sticks and clubs or whatever else they had with them. There was such a bonging and donging and horrible hammering in the great silence that Ronia screamed, afraid for her life.

When she screamed, the dwarfs stopped banging. The new sound she heard was even worse. They had begun to climb up the boulder, pressing in from all sides in the darkness. She could hear the scrape of their feet and their muttering voices: "Gray dwarfs all, bite and strike!"

Then Ronia screamed still louder in her despair and swung wildly about her with the leather bag. They would soon be on top of her, and they would bite her to death, she knew. Her first day in the forest would be her last.

But at that very moment she heard a yell; only Matt could roar so terribly. Yes, there he came, her Matt, with all his robbers, their torches flaring among the trees, and Matt's bellow echoing through the forest: "Be off, gray dwarfs! Go before I slaughter you!"

And then Ronia heard the thudding of small bodies throwing themselves off the boulder, and in the light of the torches she could see them too—little gray dwarfs fleeing in the darkness and vanishing.

She sat on the leather bag and slid down the steep boulder. Matt was there in an instant, catching her in his arms, and she wept into his beard as he carried her home to Matt's Fort.

"Now you know what gray dwarfs are," said Matt when they were sitting in front of the fire, warming Ronia's cold feet.

"Yes, now I know what gray dwarfs are," said Ronia.

"But what you don't know is how to deal with them," Matt said. "If you're frightened, they can feel it a long way off. That's when they get dangerous."

"Yes," said Lovis, "that's true of all sorts of things. So the safest thing is not to be frightened in Matt's Forest."

"I'll remember that," Ronia said.

Matt sighed and hugged her tightly. "But you do remember what I told you to watch out for?"

Yes, she remembered that. And in the days that followed, Ronia watched out for what was dangerous and practiced not being frightened. She was to be careful not to fall into the river, Matt had said, so she hopped, skipped, and jumped warily over the slippery stones along the riverbank, where the river rushed most fiercely. She was to stay by the waterfalls. To reach them, she had to climb down Matt's Mountain, which fell in a sheer drop to the river. That way she could also practice not being frightened. The first time it was difficult; she was so frightened that she had to shut her eyes. But bit by bit she became more daring, and soon she knew where the crevices were, where she could place her feet, and where she had to cling with her toes in order to hang on and not pitch backward into the rushing water.

What luck, she thought, to find a place where she could both watch out that she didn't fall in *and* practice not being frightened!

So her days passed. Ronia watched out and practiced more than Matt and Lovis knew, and in the end she was like a healthy little animal, strong and agile and afraid of nothing. Not of gray dwarfs, not of wild harpies, not of getting lost in the forest, and not of falling into the river. So far she had not begun to watch out for Hell's Gap, but she planned to start soon.

Besides that, she had explored Matt's Fort right up to the parapets. She found her way into all the deserted rooms, where no one ever set foot, and she did not lose her way in underground passages, dark pits, and cellar vaults. The secret passages of the fortress and the secret paths of the forest—she knew them all now. But it was the forest she loved best, and there she ran free as long as the day lasted.

When evening came and darkness fell and the fire was burning on the hearth in the stone hall, she would come home tired after all her watching out and practicing. That was when Matt and his robbers came back, too, from their expeditions, and Ronia sat in front of the fire with them and sang their robbers' songs. But of their robbers' life she knew nothing. She saw them come riding home in the evening with goods on their horses' backs, all kinds of goods in sacks and leather bags and chests and boxes. But no one had told her where it all came from, and she wondered about it no more than she wondered where the rain came from. Things were just *there*—she had noticed that before.

Sometimes she heard them talking about Borka robbers, and then she remembered that she was supposed to watch out for them too. But she had not seen any yet.

"If Borka were not such a scoundrel, I'd almost feel sorry for him," Matt said one evening. "The soldiers hunt him in Borka's Wood—he isn't left in peace for a moment these days. And they will soon smoke him out of his robbers' den—yes, yes, he's a dirty devil, so it doesn't matter, but all the same . . ."

"The Borka robbers are all dirty devils, the lot of them," said Noddle-Pete, and everyone agreed with him.

Wasn't it lucky that Matt's robbers were so much better, Ronia thought. She looked at them as they sat at the long table slurping up their soup. They were bearded and unwashed and noisy and wild, but no one was going to call them dirty devils in her hearing. Noddle-Pete and Shaggy, Pelle and Fooloks, Jutto and Jep, Knuckles and Knott, Tapper and Torm, Bumper and Little-Snip—they were all her friends and would go through hell and high water for her sake, as she well knew.

"Glad I am to be in Matt's Fort," said Matt. "We're as safe here as the fox in its lair and the eagle in its nest. If any soldiers are foolish enough to come here looking for trouble, they'll be sorry!"

"We'll send them straight to hell," Noddle-Pete said happily. All the robbers agreed and laughed at the very thought of the fools who might try to get into Matt's Fort. There it stood on top of the cliff, inaccessible from every side. Only on the south side a narrow little bridle path zigzagged down the mountain and disappeared into the forest below. But on three sides Matt's Fort had its sheer drop—what fool would attempt to climb there? the robbers jeered. For they had no idea where Ronia went to practice not being frightened.

"And if they come up the bridle path, they'll be stopped dead at the Wolf's Neck," said Matt. "We can hold them there by rolling rocks at them. And other things too, for that matter!"

"Other things too, for that matter," Noddle-Pete echoed, sniggering as he thought of the way they could stop the soldiers at the Wolf's Neck. "I've caught many a wolf there in my day," he added, "but I'm too old now and won't be catching anything but my own fleas, oh, ho, ho, yes!"

Ronia knew it was sad for Noddle-Pete to be so old, but she did not understand why soldiers and fools would come and make trouble at the Wolf's Neck. In any case, she was sleepy and could not be bothered thinking about it. Instead she crept onto her bed and lay awake there until she had heard Lovis sing the Wolf's Song, as she did every evening when it was time for the robbers to leave the fire and go to their bedrooms. Only Ronia, Matt, and Lovis slept in the stone hall. Ronia liked lying in her bed and watching the fire flare up and die through the gap between the curtains while Lovis sang. As long as Ronia could remember, she had heard her mother singing the Wolf's Song at night. That meant it was time to sleep, but she thought happily before she closed her eyes, Tomorrow I'll be getting up again!

And up she sprang, as soon as a new day dawned. Whatever the weather, she would be out in the forest, and Lovis gave her bread in the leather bag to take along.

"You're a storm-night child," said Lovis, "and a witch-night child, too, and it's well-known that they can easily turn into little savages. But just you take care that the harpies don't catch you!"

More than once Ronia had seen wild harpies soaring over the woods, and she had crept hurriedly away to hide. The harpies were the most dangerous of all the dangerous things in Matt's Forest—you had to watch out for them if you wanted to go on living, Matt had told her. And it was mostly because of them that he had kept Ronia at home in the fort for so long. Beautiful, mad, and ferocious, the harpies were. With stony eyes they searched the forest for something to tear with their sharp claws until it bled.

But no wild harpies could scare Ronia away from her paths and places where she lived her lonely forest life. Yes, she was lonely, but she missed no one in particular. Whom could she miss? Her days were full of life and pleasure, but they passed so quickly. The summer was over; it was autumn now.

The wild harpies always grew madder still when autumn came. One day they chased Ronia through the forest until she felt that things were getting really dangerous. Of course she could run like a fox, and of course she knew every hiding place in the forest, but the harpies pursued her stubbornly, and she heard their strident cries, "Ho, ho, pretty little human, blood will run now, ho, ho!"

She dove into the pool and swam underwater to the other side, then crawled out and hid under a thick fir tree. And she could hear the harpies searching and screaming in their rage.

"Where is the little human, where is she, where is she? Come out and we'll tear you and we'll scratch you! Blood will run, ho, ho!"

Ronia stayed in her hiding place until she saw the harpies disappearing over the treetops. She did not very much want to stay in the wood any longer just now. But there were many hours before nightfall and the Wolf's Song, so it crossed her mind that now was the time to do what she had planned for so long. She would get up on the roof and look for Hell's Gap.

She had heard many times the story of how Matt's Fort had split in two on the night she was born. Matt never tired of telling it.

"Death and destruction, what a crack! You should have heard it—well, of course you did, poor little newborn babe that you were. Bang! We had two forts instead of one, with a chasm in between. And never forget what I told you—watch out for Hell's Gap!"

And that was exactly what she was going to do. It was the best thing she could do while the harpies went mad out there in the forest.

She had often been on the roof but had never gone near the

perilous chasm that opened so sharply without any protective parapet. Now she crawled forward on her stomach and peered into the depths—oof, it was worse than she had thought!

She picked up one of the loose stones lying along the edge and dropped it, and she shivered when she heard the stone landing far, far below. The sound was so muffled and so faraway—yes, this really was a hole to watch out for! But the gap that separated the two halves of the fort was not particularly wide. One good jump would get you across it! But surely no one would be that crazy. No, but perhaps it would be a good way to watch out and practice in her usual fashion. Once again she looked down into the chasm—oof, how deep! Then she looked around for the best place to make her leap. And then she saw something that almost made her fall into Hell's Gap with surprise.

A little way off on the other side of the chasm, someone was sitting, someone about her own size, dangling his legs over Hell's Gap.

Ronia knew that she was not the only child in the world. She was simply the only child in Matt's Fort and Matt's Forest. But Lovis had said that there were plenty of children in other places, and of two kinds: those who would turn into Matts when they were big, and those who would turn into Lovises. Ronia herself would turn into a Lovis, but she knew in her heart that the one who was sitting dangling his legs over Hell's Gap would turn into a Matt.

He had not spotted her yet. Ronia watched him sitting there and laughed to herself because he was there.

Three

THEN HE CAUGHT SIGHT OF HER, AND HE LAUGHED, TOO.

"I know who you are," he said. "You're that robber's daughter who runs in the woods. I saw you there once."

"Who are you?" asked Ronia. "And how in the world did you get here?"

"I am Birk Borkason, and I live here. We moved in last night."

Ronia stared at him. "Who's we?"

"Borka and Undis and me and our twelve robbers."

It was a little time before she could take in the incredible words, but at last she said, "Do you mean that the whole of the north fort is full of dirty devils?"

He laughed. "No, there are only decent Borka robbers here. But over there where you live it's stuffed full of dirty devils—that's what they always say."

So that was what they always said! She began to boil. But there was worse to come.

"In any case," said Birk, "this isn't the north fort any more. Since last night it's called Borka's Keep—you just remember that!"

Ronia gasped with rage. Borka's Keep! That really was enough to choke you! What rogues they were, those Borka robbers! And that rascal grinning over there was one of them!

"Death and destruction," she said. "You wait until Matt hears about this, then you'll see all the Borka robbers scattered with one blow!"

"That's what you think," said Birk.

But Ronia was thinking of Matt, and she shivered. She had seen him beside himself with rage and knew what it was like. Now Matt's Fort was going to split in two all over again, she realized, and the thought made her groan.

"What's the matter with you?" Birk asked. "Don't you feel well?"

Ronia did not answer. She had heard enough now, enough of rascally talk and impudence. Something would have to be done. Matt's robbers would be home soon, and then, death and destruction, every dirty little devil of a Borka robber would be out of Matt's Fort faster than he came in!

She got up to go. But then she saw what Birk was going to do. He was getting ready to fly across Hell's Gap! He was standing on the other side, directly opposite her, and now he was beginning to run.

She screamed, "If you come here, I'll give you such a punch your nose will fall off!"

"Ha, ha," said Birk, and leaped. He was over the chasm. "Follow that if you can!" he said with a grin.

He shouldn't have said that; it was more than she could stand. All right, he and his dirty boots had planted themselves on Matt's Fort, but no Borka robber was going to go around performing leaps that one of Matt's robbers couldn't imitate!

And she did. She herself did not know how it happened, but suddenly she was flying across Hell's Gap and had landed on the other side.

"You're not so bad," said Birk, and a second later he had jumped after her.

But Ronia had not waited for him. With another leap she flew back across the chasm. He could stand there staring at her as long as he liked!

"You were going to punch me—why didn't you?" Birk said. "I'm coming!"

"So I see," said Ronia. And he came. But she did not wait for him this time, either. Once again she jumped, and she intended to go on jumping until she had no breath left in her body, if necessary, in order to get away from him.

Then neither of them spoke any more. They simply jumped. Frantically and furiously, they jumped to and fro across Hell's Gap. Nothing was heard but their panting breath. Only the crows sitting on the parapets cawed from time to time. Otherwise, everything was deadly silent. It was as if the whole of Matt's Fort were sitting there on its peak, holding its breath, waiting for something truly terrible to happen at any minute.

Yes, soon we'll both finish up in Hell's Gap, Ronia thought. But then at least there will be an end to this everlasting leaping!

There came Birk, flying across the chasm again, straight toward her, and she got ready to jump back. She no longer had any idea how many times she had jumped—it felt as if she had never done anything but jump back and forth across ravines to escape from Borka riffraff.

Then she saw Birk slip on a loose stone lying on the edge, just where he had landed, and she heard him yell before he vanished into the depths.

After that she heard only the crows. She shut her eyes and wished that this day had never happened. That Birk had not existed. And that they had never jumped.

Finally she wriggled forward on her stomach and looked down into the chasm. And there she saw Birk. He was standing on something right beneath her—a stone or a beam or whatever it was that was sticking out from the shattered walls. There was just enough room for his feet, but no more. There he stood, with the depths of Hell's Gap beneath him, his hands fumbling wildly for a hold, anything that could keep him from tumbling into the abyss. But he knew, and Ronia knew too, that without help he could not get out. He would have to stand there until he could stand no more—they both knew it—and then there would no longer be a Birk Borkason.

"Hang on," said Ronia.

And he answered with a little grin, "Well, there's not much else I can do here!"

But he was afraid; you could see that.

Ronia tore off the braided leather rope she always carried rolled in a ball on her belt. It had helped her many times with all her climbing and clambering in her forest life. Now she made a big loop at one end of the rope and tied the other end around her body. Then she lowered the rope to Birk. She saw the gleam of hope in his eyes as the rope came dangling down over his head. Yes, it was just as long as he needed, she saw, and that was just as well for this Borka rogue!

"Get this around you if you can," she said. "Then you can start climbing when I tell you to—but not before!"

The storm that had struck on the night she was born had torn a block of stone out of the parapet. By a stroke of luck it lay not far from the edge of the chasm. Ronia lay down flat on her stomach behind the great stone, and then she called, "Start now!"

And at once she felt the rope tighten around her waist. It hurt. Every tug on the rope as Birk climbed made her gasp with pain.

Soon I'm going to split in half just like Matt's Fort, she thought, and set her teeth to keep from screaming.

Then, suddenly, the strain was gone and there was Birk looking down at her. She continued to lie there, wondering if she was still able to breathe. And he said, "So that's where you are!"

"Yes, that's where I am," said Ronia. "Done enough jumping now?"

"No, I'll have to jump once more. To get to the right side. I've got to go home to Borka's Keep, you know."

"Take off my leather rope first," Ronia said, getting up. "I don't want to stay tied to you any longer than I have to."

He pulled off the rope. "No, of course not," he said. "But after this perhaps I'm tied to you all the same. Without a rope."

"Not on your life," said Ronia. "You and your Borka's Keep! Get out of here!"

She clenched her fist and punched him right on the nose.

He laughed. "Don't you do that again—take my advice! But it was nice of you to save my life, and I thank you for it!"

"Get out of here, I said," said Ronia, and ran off without looking around.

But just as she reached the stone steps that led down from the parapet into Matt's Fort, she heard Birk shout, "Hey, robber's daughter, I'll be seeing you!"

She turned her head and saw him gather himself for his last leap.

"I hope you fall in again, dirty devil!" she shouted back.

It was even worse than she had expected. Matt fell into such a rage that even his robbers were frightened.

But at first no one would believe her, and for once Matt was angry with her.

"A bit of lying and pretending may be fun sometimes. But you've got to stop this make-believe. Borka robbers in Matt's Fort, indeed! What rubbish! It makes my blood boil even though I know it's a lie."

"It's not a lie," said Ronia. And once again she tried to tell him what she had learned from Birk.

"You're lying," Matt said. "In the first place Borka hasn't got a boy. He can't have any children—that's what they've always said."

All the robbers sat there silent, not daring to speak. But at last Fooloks opened his mouth.

"Well, but they do say he has a boy, all the same. They say

Undis gave birth to him in sheer terror on the night there was such a bad storm. When we got Ronia, remember?"

Matt's eyes widened. "And no one told me! What other deviltry is there that I should know?"

He looked around furiously, and with a bellow he grasped two beer tankards, one in each fist, and flung them at the wall, making the beer gush out.

"And now Borka's snake spawn is taking his ease on the roof of Matt's Fort? And you, Ronia, have talked to him?"

"He talked to me," said Ronia.

With another yell Matt picked up the leg of lamb that had been served on the long table and flung it at the wall so hard that the grease flew.

"And that snake spawn claimed, you say, that his heathen dog of a father has moved into the North Fort with the whole of his robber scum?"

Ronia was afraid that if Matt had to listen to much more, he would be so furious he would lose his wits. But fury was needed if the Borka robbers were to be thrown out, so she said, "Yes, and now it's called Borka's Keep, just remember that!"

With a third yell Matt picked up the soup cauldron that was hanging over the fire and flung it at the wall in a shower of soup.

Lovis had sat silently listening and watching. Now she was angry and it showed. She picked up a basket of eggs, freshly gathered from the chicken run, took them to Matt, and said, "Here you are. But you'll have to clean up after yourself, remember!"

Matt took the eggs and with fearful howls flung them at the wall one by one until the place was running with yolk.

And then he cried, "Safe as the fox in its lair and the eagle in its nest—that's what I said. And now . . ."

Big as he was, he threw himself on the floor, and there he lay, crying and shouting and cursing, until Lovis was sick and tired of it.

"Now, that's enough," she said. "If you've got lice in your coat, roaring won't get rid of them. Get up and do something about it!"

The robbers were already sitting hungrily around the table. Lovis picked up the lamb from where it lay on the floor and wiped it off a little.

"It's probably only a bit more tender," she said comfortingly, and began to carve thick slices for all her robbers.

Matt got to his feet sullenly and took his seat at the table with the others. But he did not eat. He sat with his dark, tousled head in his hands and growled under his breath, sometimes giving a sigh so huge that it could be heard all around the stone hall.

Then Ronia went over to him, put her arms around his neck, and laid her cheek against his.

"Don't be sad," she said. "All you have to do is kick them out!"

"And that may be hard," said Matt heavily.

They sat in front of the fire all evening, trying to puzzle out what to do. How to get lice out of your coat, or rather how to get Borka robbers out of Matt's Fort when they had gotten a firm hold—that was what Matt wanted to know. But first and foremost he wanted to know how those snakes in the grass, those thieving rats, had managed to get into the North Fort without a single one of Matt's robbers noticing anything. Everyone who wanted to reach Matt's Fort on horseback or on foot had to pass through the Wolf's Neck, and a watch was kept there day and night. And yet no one had seen hide or hair of a Borka robber.

Noddle-Pete laughed scornfully. "Well, what did you think, Matt? That they'd come strolling through the Wolf's Neck and tell the guard, sweet as you please, 'Step aside, friend, we're planning to move into the North Fort this very night!'?"

"So which way did they come, if you know so much about it?"

"Well, not through the Wolf's Neck and the big fortress gate, by all accounts," said Noddle-Pete. "From the north side, of course, where we haven't got a guard."

"No, why should we keep a guard there? There's no entrance to the fort, and just a sheer rock wall besides. Do you think they're like flies who can climb straight up into the air? And then wriggle in through one or two narrow arrow slits?"

Then something suddenly occurred to him, and he looked at Ronia, his eyes narrowed. "What were you doing up on the roof anyway?"

"I was watching out that I didn't fall into Hell's Gap," said Ronia.

She was sorry now that she had not asked Birk a few questions. Perhaps he would have told her how the Borka robbers had managed to get into the North Fort. But it was too late to think of that now.

Matt set guards for the night, not only at the Wolf's Neck but on the roof as well.

"Borka's nerve is just too much," he said. "At any moment he'll come rushing over Hell's Gap like a wild bull and drive us out of Matt's Fort, lock, stock, and barrel."

He picked up his beer tankard and flung it at the wall so hard that the beer splashed all over the stone hall.

"I'm going to bed now, Lovis! Not to sleep. But to think and to curse, and woe betide anyone who disturbs me!"

Ronia lay awake that night too. Everything had suddenly turned so wrong and miserable. Why should that be? That Birk—after all, she had been pleased when she first saw him! And now, when she had met someone of her own age at last, why did it have to be a nasty little Borka robber?

Four

Ronia woke up early the next morning. Her father was already eating his porridge, but he was making slow progress. He would lift the spoon glumly to his mouth, but sometimes he forgot to open it. He wasn't getting much porridge down, and was no better when Little-Snip, who had been standing guard at Hell's Gap that night with Bumper and Shaggy, suddenly came rushing into the stone hall, shouting, "Borka is waiting for you, Matt! He's standing there on the other side of Hell's Gap and carrying on, and he wants to talk to you immediately!"

Then Little-Snip jumped back hastily, which was clever of him, because the next second the wooden platter with Matt's porridge on it flew past his ear and hit the wall, splashing porridge all over everything.

"You'll clean up after yourself!" Lovis reminded him sternly, but Matt was not listening to her.

"So Borka wants to talk to me! Death and destruction, so he shall, and after that he won't be doing much talking for quite a long time! If ever," said Matt, clenching his teeth till they squeaked.

Now all the robbers were crowding into the room from their bedrooms, eager to know what was going on.

"Swallow your porridge as if the place were on fire," said Matt, "because we're about to take a wild bull by the horns and throw him into Hell's Gap!"

Ronia jumped into her clothes. It did not take long, because all she had to do was to pull a short foal-skin tunic over her shift, with trousers to match. And she always went barefoot, until the snow came, so no time had to be wasted on boots or slippers when she was in a hurry.

If only everything had been as usual, she would soon have been out in the woods. But nothing was as usual any more, and she had to go up on the roof with them to see what was going to happen.

Matt urged his robbers on, and with their mouths still full of porridge, all of them marched determinedly up the stone steps of the fort to the roof. Only Noddle-Pete stayed alone by his porridge platter, fretting bitterly because he could no longer join in when there was some fun in the offing.

"Too many steps in this house," he muttered, "and too rickety legs, for that matter."

It was a clear, cold morning. The first red glow of the sun lit the deep forests around Matt's Fort. Ronia could see it over the parapet. She would have liked to be down there, in her own quiet green world— not here by Hell's Gap, where Matt's robbers and Borka's robbers now stood arrayed, glaring at each other straight across the chasm that separated them.

I see, so that's what he looks like, the snake in the grass, she thought when she saw Borka standing there, so bold and bare-faced in front of his robbers. But he was not as tall and as handsome as Matt; that was a good thing, she thought. He looked strong, though; there was no denying that. He might be short, but he was broad-shouldered and powerful, with tufts of red hair sticking out in all directions. Beside him stood someone else with red hair, although it lay like a smooth copper helmet on his head. Yes, there was Birk, apparently enjoying the scene. He gave her a secret wave, just as though they were old friends. So that was what *he* thought, the thieving dog!

"It's a good thing you came so uncommonly fast," said Borka.

Matt gave his enemy a black look. "I would have come before," he said, "but there was something I had to finish first."

"What sort of thing?" asked Borka civilly.

"A poem I was making up early this morning. 'Lament for a Dead Borka Robber,' it's called. Undis might get a bit of comfort from it when she becomes a widow!"

Perhaps Borka had thought that Matt could be reasoned with and that there would be no more quarreling about the matter of Borka's Keep. But he had made a terrible mistake there, Borka realized now, and he began to get angry.

"You should be thinking more about comforting Lovis, who has to put up with you and your big mouth all the time," he said.

Undis and Lovis, the two in need of comfort, stood each on her side of Hell's Gap, arms folded across their breasts, and looked each other straight in the eyes. They looked as if they could get on quite well without any comfort.

"Now you listen to me, Matt," said Borka. "There was no staying in Borka's Wood any longer. Soldiers are swarming there like flies, and I had to take my wife and child and all my robbers somewhere."

"Maybe so," said Matt. "But just stealing yourself a place to live, slap-bang, without asking, is something no one with a sense of shame would do."

"Strange talk from a robber," said Borka. "Haven't you always taken what you liked without asking?"

"Hmm," said Matt. He had no answer to that, but Ronia could not think why. She would have to find out what Matt had taken without asking.

"Talking of one thing and another," Matt said, after a short silence, "it would be interesting to hear how you got in, because then we can throw you out the same way."

"That's enough talk about throwing out," said Borka. "How we got in? Well, you see, we have a little monkey here who can climb the steepest walls with a long, strong rope like a tail behind him."

He patted Birk's red topknot, and Birk smiled.

"And then the little monkey tied the rope on good and tight up there so we could all climb up after him. And after that all we had to do was walk straight into the keep and start organizing ourselves a regular robbers' den."

Matt ground his teeth for a time while he pondered this. Then he said, "As far as I know there is no entrance on the north side."

"As far as you know—there's not much you know or remember

about this fortress, although you've been living here all your life! You see, in the days when it was more of a gentleman's home than now, the maids had to have a little door where they could go out and feed the pigs. Surely you at least remember where the old pigsty used to be when you were a child. Where you and I used to catch rats until your father found us and boxed my ears so hard I thought my skull was going to burst."

"Yes, my father did many good things," said Matt. "He kept all the Borka snakes in the grass in their place when he came across them."

"Yes, indeed," said Borka. "And it was that bully who taught me that every member of Matt's clan was my enemy, alive or dead. Before that I had scarcely realized that we belong to different clans, you and I, and I don't think you realized it either!"

"But I do now," said Matt. "And now there will either be a lament for a dead Borka robber or else you and your rabble will leave Matt's Fort by the way you came."

"There may well be laments of one kind or another," said Borka. "But I've made a home in Borka's Keep now, and here I stay."

"We'll soon see how things turn out," said Matt, and all his robbers growled indignantly. They wanted to stretch their bows at once, but the Borka robbers were armed too, and a battle at Hell's Gap could only end badly for all of them, as both Matt and Borka realized. So they parted now, after abusing each other one last time as a matter of form.

Matt did not look exactly like a conqueror when he returned to the stone hall, nor did any of his robbers. Noddle-Pete surveyed them in silence, then smiled his sly, toothless smile.

"That wild bull," he said, "the one you were going to take by the horns and heave into Hell's Gap—I suppose that was a crash that rumbled all around Matt's Fort?"

"Eat your porridge, if you can chew it, and leave wild bulls to me," said Matt. "I'll deal with them when the time comes."

But since at the moment the time did not seem to have come, Ronia hurried back to her woods. The days were growing shorter now; the sun would set in a few hours, but until then she wanted to be in her forest and by her lake. There it lay in the sunshine, glowing like warmest gold. But Ronia knew that the gold was deceptive and the water ice-cold. All the same, she quickly took off her clothes and dove in. She let out a shriek at first, but then she laughed with pleasure and swam and dove until the cold drove her out. Her teeth chattering, she slipped her tunic on again, but it did not help; she would have to run to get warm.

She ran like a troll between the trees and over boulders until the chill left her body and her cheeks were glowing. After that she went on running just to feel how easy it was. Shouting with joy, she came shooting out between a couple of close-growing firs and ran straight into Birk. Then rage welled up in her again. She could no longer have any peace even in the forest!

"Look where you're going, robber's daughter," said Birk. "Are you really in that much of a hurry?"

"What kind of hurry I'm in has nothing to do with you," she snapped, and she ran on. But then she slowed down. It had occurred to her that she could steal back and see what Birk was doing in her woods.

He was squatting outside the den where her fox family lived.

That annoyed her even more, because, after all, they were *her* foxes. She had been following them ever since the cubs had been born that spring. Now the cubs were big but still playful. They leaped and bit and fought each other outside the den, while Birk sat and watched them. His back was toward her, but in some strange way he knew that she was behind him, and he called out without turning, "What do you want, robber's daughter?"

" I want you to leave my fox cubs alone and get out of my woods!"

Then he got up and came toward her. "Your fox cubs! Your woods! Fox cubs belong to themselves—don't you know that? And they live in the foxes' wood, which is the wolves' and bears' and elk's and wild horses' wood too. And the owls' and the buzzards' and the wood pigeons' and the hawks' and the cuckoos' wood. And the snails' and the spiders' and the ants' wood."

"I know all the living things in these woods," said Ronia, "so don't think you have to teach me anything!"

"Then you know that it's also the wild harpies' and the gray dwarfs' and the rumphobs' and the murktrolls' wood!"

"Tell me something I don't know," said Ronia, "something I don't know better than you. Otherwise shut up!"

"In any case, it's my wood! And your wood, robber's daughter—yes, your wood too! But if you want it for yourself alone, then you're sillier than I thought when I first saw you."

He glared at her, his blue eyes dark with resentment. He did not think much of her, she could see, and it pleased her. He could think what he liked; she wanted to go home now and not have to see him any more.

"I'm happy to share the woods with the foxes and owls and spiders, but not with you," she said, and went.

Then she saw the mist coming over the forest. It rose, thick and gray, from the ground and rolled in among the trees. A moment later the sun had vanished and the golden gleam had gone. Now you could see neither stick nor stone. But she was not afraid. She could feel her way back to Matt's Fort even through the thickest fog, and she would certainly be home before Lovis sang the Wolf Song.

But what about Birk? Perhaps he knew all the paths and tracks in Borka's Wood, but here in Matt's Wood he was not so much at home. Well, then, he could stay there with the foxes, she thought, until a new day dawned without mist.

Then she heard him calling out of the thickening haze, "Ronia!"

There, now he knew her name too! Now she was no longer just a robber's daughter.

Once again he called. "Ronia!"

"What do you want?" she shouted. But he had already caught up with her.

"This mist scares me a little," he said.

"I see—you're frightened of not getting home to your thieving people? Then you'd better share the foxes' lair with them, since you're so fond of sharing!"

Birk laughed. "You're harder than stone, robber's daughter! But you can find your way to Matt's Fort better than I can. May I hold on to the edge of your tunic until we're out of the woods?"

"That you can't," said Ronia, but she untied her leather rope, the one that had saved him once before, and handed him one end.

"Here! But you'd better keep a rope's length away from me—I'm warning you!"

"As you like, cross robber's daughter," said Birk.

And so their journey began. The fog closed in on them, and they walked in silence—a rope's length apart, as Ronia had decreed.

They must not leave the path now. Any wrong step could lead them astray in the fog, Ronia knew. But she was not afraid. She felt her way forward with hands and feet. Stones, trees, and bushes were her signposts. They moved slowly, but she would still be home before Lovis sang the Wolf Song. There was no need for her to be frightened.

But she had never made as strange a journey. It was as if all the living things in the woods had fallen silent and died, and it made her feel uneasy. Were these her woods, the woods she knew and loved? Why were they so silent and menacing now? And what was that hiding in the mist? There was something there, something unknown and dangerous; she did not know what. And that scared her.

I'll be home soon, she thought to console herself. Soon I'll be lying in my bed, listening to Lovis singing the Wolf Song.

But it was no use. The fear rose in her, and she was more frightened than she had ever been before in her life. She called to Birk, but her voice was the merest squeak. It sounded so awful that it frightened her still more. I'm going to lose my wits this way, she thought; it will be the end of me!

Then, from deep in the thickest mist, there came soft, sweetly plaintive notes—a song, and it was the most wonderful song. She had never heard anything like it. Oh, how lovely it was, how it filled her forest with its beauty! And it took away all fear; it comforted her. She stood still and let herself be comforted. How beautiful it was! And how the song charmed and enticed her! Yes, she could feel that those who sang it wanted her to leave the path and follow the enchanting music into the darkness.

The song grew louder. It made her heart shake, and all of a sudden she had forgotten the Wolf Song awaiting her there at home. She had forgotten everything; all she wanted was to go to those who were calling her from the mist.

"Yes, I'm coming," she cried, and took a few steps off the path. But then came a tug on the leather rope so fierce that she fell headlong.

"Where are you going?" cried Birk. "If you let yourself be tempted away by the Unearthly Ones, you are lost—you know that!"

The Unearthly Ones—she had heard about them. She knew that they came up into the woods from their dark places underground only when the fog closed in. She had never met any of their people, but she wanted to follow them now wherever they went. She wanted to live with their songs, even if it meant spending the rest of her life underground.

"Yes, I'm coming," she called again, and tried to go. But Birk was there now, holding her fast.

"Let me go!" she shouted, striking out wildly. But he held her fast.

"Don't upset yourself," he said. But she could not hear him because of the song. It was so strong now, filling the whole forest with its resonance and herself with a longing that was impossible to resist.

"Yes, I'm coming," she called for a third time, and she struggled to free herself from Birk. She hit and scratched and screamed and cried and bit his cheek hard. But he held her fast.

He held her fast for a long time, and suddenly the fog lifted as swiftly as it had come. At that same moment the song died. Ronia looked around her, as if newly awakened from a dream. She saw the path that led home and the red sun sinking behind the wooded ridges. And Birk. He was standing there, right beside her.

"A rope's length away, I said," she reminded him. Then she saw his bloody cheek and asked, "Did the fox bite you?"

Birk did not answer. He rolled up the leather rope and gave it back to her.

"Thank you! I can find my own way home to Borka's Keep now."

Ronia peeped at him under her bangs. It was suddenly difficult to think really badly of him; she did not know why.

"Be gone then," she said kindly, and off she ran.

Five

THAT EVENING RONIA SAT IN FRONT OF THE FIRE WITH HER FATHER for a time, and then she remembered what it was she wanted to know.

"What is it that you have taken without asking? As Borka said?"

"Hmm," said Matt. "I was so afraid you wouldn't find your way home in the fog, my Ronia."

"But I did," Ronia said. "Listen, what is it that you have taken without asking?"

"Look there," said Matt, pointing excitedly into the fire. "Don't you see? It looks just like an old man! It looks like Borka. How horrid!"

But Ronia could see no sign of Borka in the fire, and she wasn't the least bit interested.

"What is it you have taken without asking?" she insisted.

When Matt did not answer, Noddle-Pete answered for him. "A lot of things! Oh, ho, oh, yes, a lot of things! I reckon it's about—"

"Stop that," Matt said angrily. "I'll deal with this myself!"

All the robbers except Noddle-Pete had already gone to their rooms. Lovis was out settling her chickens and goats and sheep for the night, so it was only Noddle-Pete who heard Matt explaining to Ronia what a robber really was—a person who took things without asking and without permission.

Matt had no need to be ashamed of that. On the contrary, he usually blustered and bragged that he was the greatest robber chieftain in all the woods and mountains. But it was a little harder now that he had to tell Ronia about it. Of course he had intended to tell her all about it sooner or later when it was necessary. But he had wanted to wait a little.

"Little innocent child that you are, my Ronia, that's why I haven't talked much about it before."

"No, you haven't said a word," Noddle-Pete assured him. "And we weren't allowed to say anything either!"

"Old man, isn't it about time you went to bed?" said Matt. But Noddle-Pete said that it wasn't. He wanted to hear this.

And Ronia understood. Now at last she understood where everything came from. All the things the robbers had on their horses' backs when they came riding home in the evening, all the goods in sacks and bundles, all the precious things in chests and boxes. They didn't grow on trees in the forest. Her father simply took them from other people.

"But don't they get terribly angry when you take their things away from them?" asked Ronia.

Noddle-Pete sniggered. "Angry fit to bust," he assured her. "Oh, dear, oh, dear, you should just hear them!"

"Old man, it would be a good thing if you finally went to bed now," said Matt.

But Noddle-Pete still would not go. "Some of them even cry," he told Ronia.

Then Matt roared, "Now be quiet! Otherwise I'll throw you out!" He patted Ronia's cheek. "You've just got to understand, Ronia! That's the way it is. That's the way it has always been. It's nothing to make a fuss about."

"No, it isn't," said Noddle-Pete. "But people never do get used to things. They go on howling and crying and swearing till it's a pleasure to hear them!"

Matt gave him an angry glare. Then he turned back to Ronia.

"My father was a robber chief, and so was my grandfather, and my great-grandfather, as you know. And I haven't let them down. I'm a robber chieftain too, the mightiest in all the woods and mountains. And that's what you're going to be, too, Ronia mine!"

"Me!" shouted Ronia. "Never! Not if they get angry and cry!"

Matt scratched his head. He was worried now. He wanted Ronia to admire and love him as much as he loved and admired her. And here she was, shouting, "Never!" and refusing to be a robber chief like her father. That made Matt unhappy. He must find a way to get her to believe that what he was doing was right and good.

"You see, Ronia darling, I take only from the rich," he protested. Then he thought for a moment.

"And I give to the poor, I really do."

Noddle-Pete sniggered. "Oh, my goodness, yes, that's true enough!

You gave that poor widow with the eight children a whole sack of flour, remember?"

"Quite so," said Matt. "I did indeed."

He stroked his black beard with satisfaction. He was very pleased now, both with himself and with Noddle-Pete.

Noddle-Pete sniggered again. "You have a good memory, you have, Matt! Let's see, that must have been ten years ago. Oh, yes, of course you give to the poor. Every ten years, give or take a year."

Then Matt roared, "If you don't go to bed now, I know someone who's going to help you get there!"

But it was not necessary, because at that moment Lovis came in and Noddle-Pete went off without assistance. Ronia went to bed, and the fire died as Lovis sang the Wolf Song. And Ronia lay there, listening and not bothering whether her father was a robber chieftain or not. He was her Matt, whatever he did, and she loved him.

That night she slept badly and dreamed of the Unearthly Ones and their enticing song, but she had forgotten all about them when she woke up.

What she remembered was Birk. In the days that followed, she sometimes thought of him and wondered how he was getting on over in Borka's Keep and how long it would be before Matt finally drove his father and their whole robber tribe out of his fort.

Matt was drawing up great new plans for action every day, but none of them was much good.

"No use," said Noddle-Pete, no matter what Matt thought of. "You'll have to be as cunning as a fox, because force won't work."

It did not suit Matt to be cunning as a fox, but he did his best.

And while this was going on, not much robbery took place. The Borka robbers had other things to think about too, and the people who had to pass through the Robbers' Walk in those days were surprised at how free from robbers it was. They could not understand why it was so peaceful. Where had all the highwaymen gone? The sheriff's men who had hunted Borka so persistently found the cave where his robbers' den had been, but it was deserted now, and empty of loot. There was no sign of Borka, and the soldiers were glad to be able to leave Borka's Wood at last, dark and cold and rainy as it was now that autumn had come. Of course they knew there were robbers far away in Matt's forest as well, but they preferred not to think about that. There was no worse place, and the robber chieftain who lived there was harder to catch than an eagle on a clifftop. They would rather leave him in peace.

Matt spent most of his time trying to work out what the Borka robbers were up to over in the North Fort and what would be the best way to get at them, so he went out scouting every day. With one or two of his men he rode to the wood on the north side, but there was no sign of the invaders. For the most part it was as silent and dead as if there were no Borka robbers there. But they had made themselves a fine, long rope ladder so they could get up and down the rock face without difficulty. Matt saw it being lowered only once. He lost his head completely and rushed forward like a madman to clamber up it. His robbers followed him, burning with lust for battle. But a shower of arrows came down from the loopholes of Borka's Keep, and Little-Snip got one in the thigh that kept him in bed for two days. Obviously the rope ladder was lowered only under strict guard.

The autumn clouds now hung heavily over Matt's Fort, and the robbers were not enjoying their inactivity. They became restless and squabbled more than usual, until Lovis could stand it no longer.

"You'll burst my eardrums soon with all your wrangling and nagging. I'll gag all of you if you don't hold your peace!"

They fell silent, and Lovis set them to useful work—clearing out and cleaning the henhouse and the sheepfold and the goat stall, all of which they heartily disliked. But no one got out of it, except Noddle-Pete and those who happened to be on guard at the Wolf's Neck and up at Hell's Gap.

Matt also did his best to keep his robbers going. He took them on elk hunts, setting out with spears and bows in the autumn woods, and Noddle-Pete smiled contentedly when they returned dragging four big elk carcasses behind them.

"Chicken soup and mutton soup and porridge don't serve a man long," he said. "Now we'll have something to chew on, and the tenderest bits go to the toothless, as everyone knows."

And Lovis roasted elk meat and smoked elk meat and salted down elk meat for the winter to supplement the roast chicken and legs of mutton.

Ronia spent her time in the woods as usual. It was very quiet there now, but she thought even the autumn woods were good to wander in. The moss was soft and green and damp under her bare feet, the smell of autumn was wonderful, and the branches of the trees glistened with moisture. It often rained, and she liked to sit hunched under a thick fir tree listening to the gentle pattering outside. Sometimes it poured down until the whole wood was running with rain, and she liked that too. There were not many animals to be seen. Her foxes stayed in their dens. But sometimes in the dusk she saw elk come trotting by, and sometimes wild horses grazing among the trees. She longed to catch a wild horse for herself and she had often tried, but without success. The wild horses were very shy and would certainly be hard to tame, but it was time she had a horse. She had told Matt so.

"Yes, when you're strong enough to catch one yourself," he had replied.

And one day I shall, she thought. I'll catch a lovely little one and take it home to Matt's Fort and tame it the way Matt did with all his horses.

Otherwise, the autumn woods were strangely deserted. All the creatures which were usually there had vanished. They had probably crept into their holes and hiding places. Sometimes, though quite rarely, harpies came swooping down from the mountains, but they were calmer now and mostly stayed up in their mountain retreats. The gray dwarfs kept away too. Just once Ronia saw one or two of them peeping out from behind a stone, but she was no longer frightened of gray dwarfs.

"Get out of here!" she shouted, and they ran off with hoarse hissing sounds.

Birk never appeared in her woods, and of course she was glad of that. Or was she? Sometimes she was not sure how she felt.

Then winter came. Snow fell, the air grew cold, and the hoarfrost transformed Ronia's forest into an ice forest, more beautiful than she could have imagined. She went skiing there, and when she turned to go home at twilight she had frost in her hair and frozen toes and fingers in spite of her leather gloves and boots. But neither cold nor snow could keep her away from the forest. The next day she was there again.

Matt was sometimes worried when he saw her rushing off down the slopes toward the Wolf's Neck, and he said to Lovis, as he had so often before, "I hope everything's all right! I hope nothing awful happens to her! I couldn't live if it did."

"What are you moaning about?" said Lovis. "That child can take care of herself better than any robber. How often do I have to tell you!"

And of course Ronia could take care of herself. But one day something happened which it was just as well Matt did not know about.

More snow had fallen in the night and covered up all Ronia's ski tracks. She would have to make new ones, and it was hard work. The cold had already laid a thin coating of ice over the snow, but it was not strong enough. She kept on breaking through it, and finally she could make no more tracks. She wanted to go home.

She had made her way up to a knoll and was going to shoot down the other side. It was a sheer drop, but she raced off fearlessly, the snow rising in clouds around her. There was a sudden dip in the ground and she flew over it, but in her flight she lost one ski, and when she landed, her foot broke through the snow into a deep hole. She saw her ski disappearing down the slope while she herself was stuck in the hole up to her knee. It made her laugh at first, but she soon stopped laughing when she realized how bad things were. She could not free herself, no matter how hard she pulled and tugged. She could hear a murmur from the hole and could not think at first what was making it. But it was not long before she saw a party of rumphobs toiling up through the snow a little way off. They were easily recognizable by their broad rumps and wrinkled little faces and scrubby hair. On the whole, rumphobs were friendly and peaceable and did no harm, but these, staring at her with their simple eyes, were obviously annoyed. They grunted and sighed, and one of them said morosely, "Woffor did un want to do that?"

And soon the others were joining in. "Woffor did un do that? Broke our roof, woffor did un?"

Ronia realized that she had stuck her foot into their underground hole. The rumphobs made these holes for themselves when they could not find a nice rotten tree to live in.

"I couldn't help it," she said. "Help me get my leg out!"

But the rumphobs just stared at her and sighed as morosely as before. "Un's stuck in t'roof, woffor did un do it?"

Ronia was growing impatient. "Help me then, and I'll go away!" But it was as if they did not hear or understand. They just stared blankly at her and ran quickly back to their hole. She could hear their irritable muttering down there, but suddenly they began to shriek and howl, as if they were pleased about something.

"She do go!" they shrieked. "She do swing there! She go!"

And Ronia could feel something hanging from her foot, something heavy.

"Li'l boy, he hang good there," shrieked the rumphobs. "See un's cradle! We mun have nasty ol' foot in roof."

But Ronia had no desire to lie in the cold and snow holding up the cradle for some stupid rumphobs. She tried again; she tugged and jerked as hard as she could to free herself. And the rumphobs cheered.

"Lil' boy, he be rockin' fine, see!"

You must not be frightened in Matt's Forest; they had been telling her that since she was small, and she had tried to arm herself against fear. But sometimes it was no good. Just now it was no good. What if she *couldn't* get free? What if she lay here and froze to death this very night! She saw the dark snow clouds over the forest; there was more snow coming, lots of snow! Perhaps she would lie hidden underneath it, dead and frozen stiff, rocking a little rumphob on her dangling foot till spring! Not till then would Matt be able to come and find his poor little daughter who had frozen to death in the wintry forest.

"No, no!" she yelled. "Help! Come and help me!"

But who was there to hear her in these empty woods? Not a soul. She knew that. But she went on shouting till she could shout no longer.

And then she heard the rumphobs grumbling again. "Un's bin and stopped rockin' now! Woffor did un?"

Then Ronia heard them no more, for she had seen the wild harpy. Like a beautiful great black bird of prey, the harpy came swooping across the forest, high up under the dark clouds, then dropped down and came in closer. Straight toward Ronia she flew, and Ronia closed her eyes. Nothing could save her now, she knew.

Screeching and cackling, the harpy landed beside her. "Pretty little human," she screamed shrilly, pulling at Ronia's hair. "Just taking a little rest, oh, yes, ho, ho!"

She cackled again, and it was the most horrid sound. "You'll have to work for us! Up in the mountains! Till the blood runs! Or else we'll scratch you, or else we'll claw you!"

The harpy began to tear and slash at Ronia with her sharp claws, and when Ronia still lay motionless, she flew into a rage.

"Do you want me to scratch and claw you?"

She bent over Ronia, her stony black eyes gleaming wickedly. Then she made another effort to get Ronia free, but no matter how she tugged and tore, it was no use, and in the end she tired of it.

"Then I'll go and fetch my sisters," she screamed. "We'll get you tomorrow. You'll never take another rest here, never, never!" And off she flew over the treetops and disappeared toward the mountain peaks.

Tomorrow when the wild harpies come, there will be nothing here but a lump of ice, Ronia thought.

There was silence now down in the rumphobs' hole. The whole forest was silent, waiting for the night to come. Ronia was not waiting for anything else herself. She lay still; she had given up struggling. It would come now, she thought, the last cold, dark, lonely night, which would put an end to her.

The snow had begun to fall, and big flakes settled softly on her face. They melted there and mixed with her tears, for she was crying now. She was thinking of Matt and Lovis. She would never see them again, and no one would ever be happy again in Matt's Fort. Poor Matt, he would lose his senses with sorrow! And there would be no Ronia there to comfort him as she used to do when he was sad. No, there was no comfort to be given now, and none to be had, none at all!

Then she heard someone speaking her name. She heard it clearly and distinctly, but she knew that it must be a dream, and that made her cry again. Never more, except in dreams, would anyone call her by name. And soon she would not even dream any longer.

But then she heard the voice once again.

"Ronia, shouldn't you go home now?"

She opened her eyes reluctantly, and there stood Birk—yes, there stood Birk, on his skis!

"I found your ski down at the bottom, and that was pure luck, because otherwise you'd have gone on lying here." He put the ski down on the snow beside her. "Need help, do you?"

Then she was crying in earnest, so loudly and so desperately that she was ashamed. She was crying so hard that she could not answer him, but when he bent down to lift her up, she flung her arms around him and muttered frenziedly, "Don't leave me! Don't ever leave me again!"

That made him smile. "No, as long as you keep a rope's length away! Let go of me and stop howling and I'll see if I can get you free."

He took off his skis, lay down beside her, and thrust his hand as far as he could into the hole. And when he had worked at it for a long time, the miracle happened. Ronia could pull her leg up—she was free!

But the rumphobs in their hole were angry, and their little one whimpered, "Woke li'l boy up, an' 'e got dirt in 's eyes, woffor did un do it?"

Ronia cried; she could not stop herself. Birk handed her the ski.

"Stop howling," he said. "Otherwise you'll never get home."

Ronia drew a deep breath. Yes, the crying was over now. She got to her feet and tested her leg to see if it would hold her.

"I've got to try," she said. "And you'll come too, won't you?"

"I'll come too," said Birk.

Ronia set off and made the run down the slope, and Birk followed her. All the time, as she skied painfully homeward in the swirling snow, she had him behind her. Time and again she had to make sure that he was still there. She was so frightened that he might suddenly disappear and leave her on her own. But he was following her, a rope's length away, until they were nearly at the Wolf's Neck. There they had to part. From there Birk would take a secret way back to Borka's Keep.

They stood silently for a time in the falling snow, trying to say good-bye. It was difficult, Ronia felt, and she wanted with all her strength to keep him there.

"Listen, Birk," she said. "I wish you were my brother."

Birk laughed. "Why shouldn't I be, if you like, robber's daughter!"

"I do like," she said. "But only if you call me Ronia."

"Ronia, sister mine," said Birk, and then he was gone in the whirling snow.

Six

IT WENT ON SNOWING THAT NIGHT OVER MATT'S FORT AND THE SURrounding woods, and even Noddle-Pete could not remember a worse snowstorm. It took four men to push back the great fortress gate enough for a man to squeeze out and dig away the worst of the drifts. Noddle-Pete stuck his nose out and saw the desolate white landscape where everything was now hidden under the snow. The Wolf's Neck was completely walled up. No one was going to be able to get through that tunneled path until spring if the winter went on as it had begun, said Noddle-Pete.

"Listen, Fooloks," he said, "if digging snow is what you like best, I can promise you much joy for quite a time."

Noddle-Pete's predictions were usually right, and he was right this time too. For a long time the snow fell day and night. The robbers dug and swore, but at least there was one thing in their favor: they no longer needed to keep watch on Borka's followers, either at the Wolf's Neck or at Hell's Gap.

"Of course, that Borka is more stupid than a pig," said Matt, "but he's not quite so impossibly stupid as to want to fight in snow up to his armpits."

Matt was not that stupid either, and in any case he was not particularly troubled about Borka just now. He had other things to think about. Ronia was ill for the first time in her life. The morning after the day in the wintry forest, which had so nearly been her last, she woke up with a high fever and felt to her astonishment that she had no desire at all to get up and start living, as she usually did.

"What's the matter with you?" shouted Matt, flinging himself on his knees by her bed. "What are you saying? You're not really ill, are you?"

He took her hand and felt how hot it was; in fact her whole body was burning, he realized, and he grew frightened. He had never seen her like this before. She had been bursting with health all her life. But here she lay now, this daughter whom he loved so much, and at once he knew. He knew what was going to happen! Ronia was going to be taken from him; she was going to die; he felt it, until his heart was sore within him. And he had no idea what to do with his terrible sorrow. He would have liked to bang his head against the wall and bellow as he used to do. But he must not terrify the poor child; at least he had sense enough for that. So he simply laid his hand on her burning forehead and murmured, "It's a good thing to keep warm, my Ronia! That's what you have to do when you're ill."

But Ronia knew her father, and in spite of the fever burning inside her she tried to comfort him.

"Don't be silly, Matt! This is nothing. It could be much worse."

It could have been so much worse that I might have lain hidden under the snow from winter to spring, she thought. Poor Matt, once again she imagined how it would have tortured him, and tears rose to her eyes. Matt saw them and thought she was lying there mourning because she was to die so young.

"My little one, you'll soon be fit again. Don't cry," he said, swallowing back his own sobs bravely. "But where's your mother?" he roared, and rushed weeping to the door.

Why was Lovis not standing ready with her soothing herbs, when Ronia's life was hanging by a hair, he would like to know!

He looked for Lovis in the sheepfold, but she was not there. The sheep bleated hungrily in their pen, but they soon realized that the right person had not arrived. For this one stood with his shaggy head bowed on the edge of the pen, crying so desperately that they were all scared to death.

Matt went on bawling until Lovis, having finished her duties with the goats and chickens, walked in through the door. Then he roared, "Woman, why are you not with your sick child?"

"Have I a sick child?" was Lovis's calm reply. "I didn't know. But as soon as I have given the sheep what they need—"

"I can do that! Go to Ronia!" he shouted, and then snuffled more quietly. "If she's still alive!"

He began to toss out bundles of aspen from their provisions, and when Lovis had gone, he fed the sheep and lamented to them, "You don't know what it's like having children! You don't know what it feels like to lose your dearest little lamb!"

He stopped suddenly, remembering that they had all had lambs in the spring. And what had become of them? Nothing but roast mutton!

Lovis gave her daughter soothing herb juices to drink, and in three days Ronia was well again, to Matt's amazement and joy. Ronia was herself again, though perhaps a little more thoughtful than before. She had done a lot of thinking during her three days in bed. What was going to happen now with Birk? She had a brother, yes, but how were they ever going to meet? It would have to be in secret; she could never tell Matt that she had a Borka for a friend. It would be like hitting him over the head with a sledgehammer, only much worse, and he would be more heartbroken and more furious than ever before. Ronia sighed. Why did her father have to be so violent about everything? No matter whether he was happy or angry, it was always the same: he was savage and stormy enough for a whole band of robbers.

Ronia was not used to lying to her father. She just kept quiet about anything she knew was going to make him sad or angry. Or both sad and angry, which he would be if she told him about Birk. But it could not be helped; now that she had a brother she wanted to be with him, even if she had to steal away to do it.

But where could she steal to in all this snow? She could not get out into the forest, because the Wolf's Neck was blocked, and in any case these winter woods scared her a little. She had had enough of them for a while.

The snowstorms continued to whine around Matt's Fort, getting a little worse all the time, and at last Ronia realized just how bad things were: she would not be able to see Birk again until spring. He was as far away from her as if there were a thousand miles between them.

It was all the snow's fault. Ronia became more and more annoyed with it with each day that passed, and the robbers loathed it as much as she did. They cast lots every morning for guard duty. Some of them had to labor up the path to the spring where they fetched the water. It was halfway to the Wolf's Neck, and it was hard work getting there, with the snow whirling around your ears, and then lugging back heavy buckets of water, enough for both men and beasts.

"You're as idle as oxen," Lovis accused the men, "except when you're fighting and robbing—then you work hard."

And the idle robbers looked forward to spring, when their robbers' life could start again. They passed the long hours of waiting by shoveling more and more snow and cutting new skis and looking after their weapons and grooming their horses and playing dice and dancing robber dances and singing robber ditties in front of the fire as they had always done.

Ronia played dice with them and sang and danced as well, but she was looking forward to spring just as much as the robbers were, and to her woods in springtime. Then at last she would see Birk again. They would be able to talk, and she could find out if he really did want to be her brother as he had promised out in the snowstorm.

But waiting was hard, and Ronia hated being shut in. It made her restless, and the days seemed long. So one day she made her way down to the underground cellar vaults where she had not been for a long time. Old dungeons were something she did not care for, and there were many of them down there, blasted into the rock wall. Of course Noddle-Pete insisted that nobody had been kept captive there since time immemorial, when great men and small kings had ruled from Matt's Fort, long before it had become a robber stronghold.

All the same, when Ronia came down into the musty cold of the vaults, she felt that something of the moaning and sighing of those long-dead prisoners still clung to the rock walls, and it gave her a creepy feeling. She lit up the darkness of the dungeons with her horn lantern, the corners where the poor wretches had lived without hope of ever again seeing the light of day. She stood quietly for a while, grieving for the cruelties that had taken place in Matt's Fort. Then, with a shudder, she pulled her wolfskin coat closer around her and trudged on through the underground passages that stretched past the dungeons under the entire fortress. She had been there with Noddle-Pete, and he was the one who had shown her what the storm had done on the night when she was born. Not content with opening up Hell's Gap, it had crushed the rock directly under the gap as well, and therefore the underground passage had caved in in the middle and filled up with rubble.

"This is the end. Here you must stop," said Ronia, just as Noddle-Pete had said when she had been there with him.

But then she began to think. On the other side of the rockfall the passage went on, she knew, for Noddle-Pete had told her that too. It had always irritated her that she could go no farther, and now more than ever, because—who could tell?—surely somewhere on the other side of all this rubble there would be Birk.

She stood gazing thoughtfully at the heaps of fallen stones. And at last her thinking was done.

For some time after that they saw little of Ronia in the stone hall. She disappeared every morning, no one knew where, and neither Matt nor Lovis wondered where she was. Of course she would be shoveling snow like all the others, they thought, and in any case they were used to her coming and going as she liked.

But Ronia was not shoveling snow. She was moving rubble until her arms and back ached. And when she tumbled into bed at night, exhausted, there was one thing she knew for sure: never again in her life was she going to move stones, big or little. But morning had scarcely dawned before she was back in the underground passage, setting to with furious energy, filling bucket after bucket with stones. She hated them, all those heaped-up stones, so much that they should have melted. But they did not; they continued to lie there, and she herself had to haul them away, bucket by bucket, and empty them in the nearest dungeon.

There came a day when the dungeon was full and the heap of stones had sunk to a point where with a bit of difficulty it should be possible to climb over to the other side—if she dared! Now Ronia knew it was time to think. Did she dare walk straight into Borka's Keep? And what would happen to her there? She did not know, but what she did know was that she was on dangerous ground. All the same, there was nothing so dangerous that she would not try it in order to reach Birk. She longed for him. How that had happened she had no idea. After all, she had detested him and wished him and all the Borka robbers at the bottom of Hell's Gap, and now here she stood, wanting only to reach the other side of the rubble and see if she could find Birk.

Then she heard something. There was someone coming on the other side. She could hear footsteps. Who could it be but a Borka robber? She held her breath and stood stock-still, not daring to move, listening and wishing she were far away before whoever was on the other side of the pile of stones discovered she was there.

Then the Borka robber began to whistle, a simple little tune she had heard before. Yes, indeed she had heard it before! Birk had been whistling it when he was struggling to free her from the rumphobs' hole. Could it be Birk in there, so close to her, or did all the Borka robbers whistle that particular tune?

She was burning to find out, but she could not very well ask; that would be dangerous. All the same, she must find out somehow who the whistler was, so she decided to whistle too, the same tune, very softly.

There was silence on the other side. For a long time it was horribly quiet, and she was making ready to rush off if an unknown Borka robber suddenly came scrambling over the rubble to get his hands on her.

But then she heard Birk's voice, low and hesitant, as if he did not know what to expect. "Ronia?"

"Birk!" she shouted, so tremendously happy that she almost lost her breath. "Birk, oh, Birk!"

Then she stopped. After a moment she said, "Is it true that you want to be my brother?"

She heard him laughing on the other side of the rubble. "My

sister," he said, "I like hearing your voice, but I would like to see you too. Are you as black-eyed as you used to be?"

"Come and see," said Ronia.

She got no further, because now she had heard something else, something that took her breath away and silenced her. She had heard the heavy cellar door, far away behind her, opening and closing again with a bang, and now someone was coming down the steps. Yes, someone was coming, and if she could not work out what to do very quickly she was lost—and so was Birk! She heard footsteps coming closer and closer. Someone was coming softly and inexorably down the long corridor. She heard and knew what it meant, yet she stood there like an idiot, motionless with terror. It was almost too late when she suddenly came back to life and whispered quickly to Birk, "Tomorrow!"

Then she ran to meet whoever was coming. Whoever he was, he must be prevented from seeing what she had been doing with the tumbled stones.

It was Noddle-Pete, and his face brightened when he saw her.

"How I've searched!" he said. "What in the name of all the wild harpies have you been doing?"

She took him briskly by the arm and turned him around before it was too late.

"You can't shovel snow all the time," she said. "Come on, I want to get out of here."

Indeed she did! It was only now that she realized what she had done. She had opened up a way into Borka's Keep—if Matt only knew! He might not have the cunning of a fox, but at least he would understand that here at last was a way of getting at Borka.

He could have worked it out for himself long ago, thought Ronia, but she was glad he had not done so. It was strange, but she no longer wanted to have the Borka robbers thrown out of Matt's Fort. They must be allowed to stay here, for Birk's sake. Birk must not be thrown out, and if she could prevent it, no one was going to get into Borka's Keep by the way she had opened up. So she must make sure now that Noddle-Pete did not start thinking any unnecessary thoughts. There he was, walking beside her, looking very knowing—though that was his usual expression. It was easy to imagine that he knew all your secrets, but however artful he was, this time Ronia was more artful still. He had not discovered her secret—not yet, at least.

"No, no, you can't shovel snow all the time," Noddle-Pete agreed. "But you can play dice night and day, don't you think, Ronia?"

"You can play dice night and day. And especially now," said Ronia, dragging him enthusiastically up the steep cellar steps.

She played dice with Noddle-Pete until it was time for the Wolf Song, but Birk was always in her thoughts.

Tomorrow! That was the last thing she thought before she fell asleep that night. Tomorrow!

Seven

AND THEN IT WAS MORNING AND SHE WAS GOING TO BIRK. SHE MUST go quickly, watching out for the brief moment when she was alone in the stone hall while all the others were about their various morning jobs. At any moment Noddle-Pete might pop up, and she wanted to avoid his questions.

I can eat just as well underground, she thought. There's no eating one's meal in peace here, anyway.

She stuffed bread hastily into her leather bag and poured milk into her wooden jar. And without being seen by anyone she made her way down to the cellar vaults. Soon she had reached the pile of stone.

"Birk," she called, afraid that he might not be there. No one answered from beyond the heaps of stone, and she felt disappointed enough to cry—what if he did not come! Perhaps he had completely forgotten, or—still worse—perhaps he had regretted their meeting. After all, she was one of Matt's robbers and an enemy of Borka; perhaps in the end he did not want to have anything to do with someone like that.

Then someone behind her gave her hair a tug. She screamed with fright. Did he have to come sneaking in again, that Noddle-Pete, and ruin everything?

But it was not Noddle-Pete. It was Birk. There he stood, laughing, and his teeth were white in the darkness. She could not see much more of him in the glow from the horn lamp.

"I've been waiting a long time," he said.

Ronia felt a little spurt of joy inside her—just think, she had a brother who would wait a long time for her sake!

"And so have I," she said. "I've been waiting ever since I got away from the rumphobs."

Then for a time they could think of nothing more to say. They just stood there, silent but very pleased to be together again.

Birk raised his tallow candle and held it up to her face.

"You've still got the black eyes," he said. "You look like you, only a little paler."

It was only then that Ronia noticed that Birk did not look like himself as she remembered him. He had grown thin; his face was haggard and his eyes very large.

"What have you been doing with yourself?" she asked.

"Nothing," said Birk, "but I haven't been eating much. Even so, I've had more than anyone else in Borka's Keep."

It was a little time before Ronia understood what he had said.

"Do you mean that you haven't any food? That you haven't enough to eat?"

"None of us has had enough to eat for a long time. All our food is running out, and if spring doesn't come soon, we'll all be done for. Just as you wanted, remember?" he said, laughing.

"That was then," said Ronia. "I didn't have a brother then. Now I have."

She opened the leather bag and gave him the bread. "Eat, if you're hungry," she said.

There was an extraordinary sound, almost like a little scream, from Birk. And he took the coarse chunks of bread, one in each hand, and ate. It was as if Ronia were not there. He was alone with his bread, gulping it down to the very last crumb. Then Ronia handed him the jar of milk, and he put it greedily to his mouth and drank until it was empty.

Afterward he looked shamefacedly at Ronia. "Shouldn't you have had this for yourself?"

"There's more at home," she said. "I'm not starving."

And in her mind's eye she saw Lovis's rich stores in the great larder: the wonderful bread, the goat cheese and soft whey cheese, and the eggs, the barrels of salted food, the smoked joints of mutton hanging from the roof, the bins full of flour and grain and dried peas, the crocks of honey, the baskets of hazelnuts and bags of herbs and leafy plants that Lovis had gathered and dried to put into the chicken soup she sometimes prepared. That chicken soup—Ronia began to feel hungry as she remembered how good it tasted after all the salted and smoked food they had to eat throughout the winter.

But where Birk lived they were starving. She could not think why.

He explained it to her. "We're poor robbers for the time being, you see. We had goats and sheep too, before we came here to Matt's Fort. Now we have nothing but our horses, and we stabled them for the winter with a farmer down beyond Borka's Forest. Thank goodness we did—otherwise we would have eaten them, as things are now. We did have a bit of flour and some turnips and peas and salt fish, but they are running out now. Oof, what a winter we've been having!"

Ronia felt as if it were her fault and the fault of Matt's Fort that Birk had had such troubles and was now so thin and hungry. But he could still laugh in spite of it all.

"Poor robbers, yes, that's what we are! Can't you smell the dirt and poverty on me?" he said with a grin. "We've scarcely any water either. We've had to melt snow, because sometimes it's been impossible to go down to the woods and dig out the stream under all the snow. And then, hauling a bucket of water up a rope ladder in a snowstorm—have you ever tried it? No, because if you had you'd know why I smell like a dirty robber!"

"Our robbers smell the same," Ronia assured him, to comfort him a little. She herself smelled quite all right, because Lovis scrubbed her in the big wooden tub in front of the fire every Saturday night and deloused her and Matt with the louse comb every Sunday morning, although Matt complained that she pulled his hair out at the same time. He did not want to be combed, but he had to put up with it.

"Twelve matted, lousy robbers are enough," Lovis had said. "I intend to comb the chief, dead or alive, as long as I can manage to lift a louse comb."

Ronia looked earnestly at Birk, standing there in the lamplight. Even if he had not been deloused, his hair still lay like a copper helmet around his head, and his head sat so handsomely on his slender neck and straight shoulders. He was a handsome brother, Ronia thought.

"It doesn't matter if you are poor and lousy and dirty," she said. "But I don't want you to be hungry."

Birk laughed. "How did you know that I was lousy—I certainly am! But I'd rather be lousy than hungry, that's for sure."

Now he was serious again. "Forget being hungry! But I could have saved a bit of bread for Undis, at all events!"

"I can get some more," Ronia said thoughtfully, but Birk shook his head.

"No, I can't take bread home to Undis without telling her where I got it. And Borka would be beside himself with fury if he found out that I was taking bread from you and had become your brother into the bargain."

Ronia sighed. She could well understand that Borka must loathe Matt's robbers as much as Matt loathed the Borka robbers, but oh, how it messed things up for her and Birk!

"We can never meet except in secret," she said sadly, and Birk agreed.

"That's true! And I hate doing things in secret."

"Me too," said Ronia. "There's nothing I hate more than old salt fish and long winters, but keeping things secret when it's just silly is even worse."

"But you'll do it all the same? For my sake? And it will be easier in spring," said Birk. "We can meet in the woods then instead of in this ice-cold hole of a cellar."

They were both so cold that their teeth chattered, and at last Ronia said, "I think I have to go now, before I freeze to death."

"But you will come back tomorrow? To your lousy brother?"

"I'll come with the louse comb and this and that," said Ronia.

And she kept her promise. Early every morning, as long as the winter lasted, she met Birk down in the cellar vaults and kept him alive with food from Lovis's larder.

Birk was sometimes ashamed of taking her gifts. "I feel as if I were stealing from you," he said.

But that made Ronia laugh. "Aren't I a robber's daughter? So why shouldn't I steal?"

In any case she knew that much of what Lovis kept in her stores had already been stolen from rich merchants traveling through the woods.

"A robber takes without asking or getting permission—that little I have finally learned," said Ronia. "And now I'm doing what I've learned. So just you eat!"

Every day she also gave him a bag of flour and a bag of peas for him to add secretly to Undis's store.

So it's come to this, she thought, I want to keep Borka robbers alive. Woe betide me if Matt ever finds out!

Birk thanked her for her generosity.

"Undis is amazed every day because there are still a few peas and a little flour left in her bins. She thinks there must be some kind of sorcery at work," Birk said, laughing in his usual way. He was a little more himself now and no longer had that famished look, which pleased Ronia greatly.

"Who knows?" said Birk. "Perhaps my mother is right about the sorcery. You do look a bit like a little harpy, Ronia."

"But nice and with no claws," said Ronia.

"Yes, as nice as nice can be! How many times do you plan to save my life, sister mine?"

"As many times as you've saved mine," she said. "The fact is, we can't manage without each other. I realize that now."

"Yes, that's true," said Birk. "So Matt and Borka can think what they like."

But Matt and Borka were not thinking about it at all, because they did not know anything about the meetings between brother and sister under the cellar vaults.

"Have you eaten enough?" Ronia asked. "I'm going to start on the louse comb now."

She lifted the comb like a weapon and advanced on him. Poor Borka robbers, they did not have even a louse comb left! But she liked feeling Birk's soft hair under her hands and combed him more often than was strictly necessary.

"I'm already so extremely deloused," said Birk, "that I think you're combing in vain."

"We shall see," said Ronia, running the comb vigorously through his hair.

Gradually the harsh winter began to turn milder. The snow melted little by little, and on a day when the midday thaw was at its height, Lovis drove the robbers out into the snow to wash themselves and get rid of the worst of the dirt. They resisted and would not go. Such things were harmful to the health, Fooloks insisted. But Lovis stood her ground. The smell of winter must go now, she said, even if every robber perished in the process. She drove them out into the snow without mercy, and soon naked, hooting robbers were rolling all over the snowy slopes down by the Wolf's Neck. They cursed loud and long over Lovis's inhuman heartlessness, but they scrubbed themselves as she had told them. They did not dare do otherwise.

Only Noddle-Pete stubbornly refused to roll in the snow. "I may die anyway," he said, "and I want to do it with the dirt I've got on me."

"Just as you like," said Lovis, "but before you do, you could at least tidy up the hair and beards of those other wild goats."

Noddle-Pete would be glad to, he said. He was skillful with the shears when there were sheep and lambs to be clipped. so he could certainly make short work of any old wild goat.

"But I'm going to leave my own two little tufts of hair alone. No unnecessary fuss, for I'll soon be under the ground," he said, stroking his bald pate contentedly.

Then Matt flung his mighty arms around Noddle-Pete and lifted him a good way off the floor. "You stop that about dying! I haven't lived a day of my earthly life without you yet, you old fool, so you can't just go and die behind my back, as you very well know!"

"We shall see, little boy, we shall see," said Noddle-Pete, looking thoroughly pleased with himself.

Lovis spent the rest of the day washing filthy robbers' clothes in the yard of the fortress, and in the wardrobe room the robbers looked for clothes to put on while their own were drying. Most were garments that Matt's grandfather had stolen and brought home in his time. How could anyone in his senses have worn getups like these? Fooloks wondered, doubtfully pulling a red shirt over his head. It was all very well for him, but it was much worse for Knott and Little-Snip, who had to be content with petticoats and corsets, since all the men's clothing had already gone when they came to look. It did not improve their tempers, but Matt and Ronia were kept amused for a long time.

Lovis served chicken soup that night to make up for everything with her robbers. They sat sulkily around the long table, scrubbed clean and cut tidy and quite unrecognizable. Even the smell was different.

But when the powerful scent of Lovis's chicken soup spread down the long table, the robbers stopped sulking. And as soon as they had eaten, they sang and danced as they used to do, though a little more tamely than usual. Knott and Little-Snip in particular avoided any of the more violent leaps.

Eight

AND THEN SPRING CAME LIKE A SHOUT OF JOY TO THE WOODS AROUND Matt's Fort. The snow melted, streaming down all the cliff faces and finding its way to the river. And the river roared and foamed in the frenzy of spring and sang with all its waterfalls a wild spring song that never died. Ronia heard it every waking hour and even in her nightly dreams. The long, terrible winter was over. The Wolf's Neck had long been free of snow. There was a turbulent stream rushing down it now, and the water splashed around the horses' hooves when Matt and his robbers came riding early one morning through the narrow pass. They sang and whistled as they rode out. Oh, ho, at last their splendid robbers' life was beginning again!

And at last Ronia was going to her woods, which she had missed so much. The moment the snow melted and all the ice thawed away, she should have been there to see what was happening in her domain, but Matt had stubbornly kept her at home. The spring forests were full of dangers, he claimed, and he would not let her go until it was time for him to set out with his robbers.

"Off you go then," he said, "and don't drown yourself in some treacherous little pool."

"Oh, yes, I shall," Ronia said. "To give you something to make a fuss about at last."

Matt gazed gloomily at her. "My Ronia," he said with a sigh. Then he flung himself into the saddle, led his robbers down the slopes, and was gone.

As soon as Ronia saw the last horse's rump disappear through the Wolf's Neck, she followed at a run. She, too, was singing and whistling as she waded in the cold water of the brook. Then she was running, running, until she reached the lake.

And there was Birk, as he had promised. He was stretched out on a flat rock in the sunshine. Ronia did not know if he was asleep or awake, so she picked up a stone and tossed it into the water to see if he heard the splash. He did, and he sprang up and came toward her.

"I've been waiting a long time," he said, and once again she felt that little spurt of joy because she had a brother who waited and wanted her to come.

And here she was now, diving headfirst into spring. It was so magnificent everywhere around her, it filled her, big as she was, and she screeched like a bird, high and shrill.

"I have to scream a spring scream or I'll burst," she explained to Birk. "Listen! You can hear spring, can't you?"

They stood silently, listening to the twittering and rushing and buzzing and singing and murmuring in their woods. There was life in every tree and watercourse and every green thicket; the bright, wild song of spring rang out everywhere.

"I'm standing here feeling the winter run out of me," said Ronia. "Soon I'll be so light I can fly."

Birk gave her a nudge. "Fly then! There are sure to be some wild harpies flying around—you can join their flock."

Ronia laughed. "Yes, I'll have to see how I get on."

But then she heard the horses. Somewhere down by the river they were coming at a full gallop, and she began to hurry.

"Come on! I'd like to catch a wild horse!"

And they ran until they saw them, hundreds of horses charging through the forest until the ground rang under their hooves.

"A bear or wolf must have scared them," said Birk. "Otherwise why would they be so frightened?"

Ronia shook her head. "They're not frightened—they're just running winter out of their bodies. But when they're tired of that and begin to graze, I'm going to catch one and take it home to Matt's Fort. I've wanted to do that for a long time."

"To Matt's Fort—what do you want a horse there for? Riding is for the woods. We might as well catch two and ride them right away."

Ronia thought it over. Then she said, "Even the Borka clan can have brains in their heads, I see. We'll do it! Come on, let's try!"

She took off her leather rope. Birk had gotten a similar one for himself, and with their snares ready they hid behind a boulder at the entrance to the glade where all the wild horses liked to graze.

They did not mind waiting at all.

"I'm enjoying just sitting here in the midst of spring," Birk said.

Ronia stole a look at him and muttered under her breath, "I like you for that, Birk Borkason!"

For a long time they sat there silently. They heard blackbirds and cuckoos singing and calling till the sound filled the sky. Newborn fox cubs scampered about outside their den a stone's throw from Ronia and Birk. Squirrels dashed to and fro in the treetops, and they saw hares come skipping over the moss, then disappear in the bushes. A snake which was soon going to have young lay peacefully in the sun quite close to them. They did not disturb her and she did not disturb them. Spring was for everyone.

"You're right, Birk," said Ronia. "Why should I take a horse away from the woods where he belongs? But I do want to ride, and now it's time."

The glade was suddenly filled with grazing horses, moving calmly about, nibbling at the fresh grass.

Birk pointed to a pair of fine young chestnut horses which were grazing together, a little removed from the herd. "What do you say to those two?"

Ronia nodded. With their ropes ready, they approached the two horses, coming up behind them softly and soundlessly, slowly, nearer and nearer. Then a little twig snapped under Ronia's foot, and at once the whole herd was alert, ready to flee. But when no danger appeared, no bears or wolves, no lynx or other enemy, they settled down again and began to graze.

The two young horses which Birk and Ronia had chosen settled down too. Now they were within touching distance. Birk and Ronia nodded to each other, the two lassos flew out at once, and the next moment all that could be heard was the wild neighing of two captured horses and the thunder of hooves as the rest of the herd fled through the forest.

They had caught two foals, two wild young stallions which kicked and reared and bit and struggled frantically to free themselves as Birk and Ronia tried to tie each of them to a tree.

They succeeded in tethering them at last, then jumped out of reach of the flying hooves. Ronia and Birk stood panting, watching the horses kick and lunge until they were dripping with foam.

"We were going to ride," said Ronia. "These two are not going to let us ride them the first time we try."

Birk had realized that too. "First we'll have to make them understand that we wish them no harm."

"I've already tried that," Ronia said, "with a bit of bread. And if I hadn't pulled my hand away as fast as I did, I'd have gone home with a couple of bitten-off fingers dangling from my belt. That wouldn't have made Matt particularly happy and cheerful!"

Birk turned pale. "Do you mean that villain snapped at you when you were giving him bread? And really *wanted* to bite you?"

"Ask him," Ronia said briefly.

She cast a dejected look at the fierce stallion as he continued to fume and rage. "Villain—that's a good name," she said. "I'll call him that."

Birk laughed. "Then you'll have to give mine a name in exchange."

"Yes, he's just as crazy," said Ronia. "You can call him Savage."

"Do you hear that, wild horses?" Birk shouted. "We've given you names. You're Villain and Savage, and you belong to us now, whether you like it or not!"

Villain and Savage did not like it; that was obvious. They continued to tear and bite at the leather thongs, and sweat ran down their sides, but they went on kicking, and their wild whinnying terrified the animals and birds for miles around.

But as the day advanced toward evening, they gradually quieted down. At last the horses were standing still, heads hanging, giving only an occasional subdued and mournful whinny.

"They must be thirsty," said Birk. "We must take them to water."

And they released their now well-behaved horses, led them to the lake, removed the leather ropes, and let them drink.

They drank for a long time. Afterward they stood still and content, gazing dreamily at Birk and Ronia.

"We've tamed them at last," Birk said delightedly.

Ronia patted her horse, looked deep into his eyes, and explained, "When I say I'm going to ride, I'm going to ride. Understand?"

Then she took a firm grip on Villain's mane and swung herself onto his back.

"Now then, Villain," she said. And then she was flying in a wide arc, headfirst into the lake. She popped up again just in time to see Villain and Savage disappear between the trees at a full gallop.

Birk gave her his hand and pulled her out. He did it silently and without looking at her. Ronia climbed out of the water, equally silent. She shook herself, drops of water flying about her, and then with a peal of laughter she said, "I won't be riding any more today!"

Birk gave a hoot of laughter too. "I won't either!"

Evening came, the sun sank, dusk fell, the dusk of a spring evening that was no more than a strange dimness between the trees and never turned into darkness and night. The woods fell silent. There was no more sound of blackbird and cuckoo. All the fox cubs crept into their lairs, all the baby squirrels and hares to their nests, the adder under her stone. All that could be heard was the owl's far-off melancholy hooting, and in a little while that too died away.

The whole wood had seemed to be sleeping. But now it awakened slowly to its twilight life. All the twilight creatures which lived there began to stir. There was a rustling and creeping and stealing among the moss. The rumphobs snuffled among the trees, shaggy murk-trolls crept behind the boulders, and gray dwarfs came crawling out of their hiding places in large troops, hissing to frighten everyone as they came out. And down from the mountains hovered the wild harpies, the cruelest and fiercest of all the forest's twilight creatures, black against the pale spring sky. Ronia saw them, and she did not like them.

"There are more goblins around here than we need! And I want to go home now, black and blue and soaked right through as I am."

"Black and blue and soaked right through you are," said Birk. "But then, you have also spent a whole day in the midst of spring."

Ronia knew she had stayed in the woods too long, and when she left Birk she tried to think how she could get around Matt and make him understand why she had had to stay out in spring until late at night.

But neither Matt nor anyone else noticed or bothered about her when she walked into the stone hall. They had other worries.

On a skin in front of the fire lay Bumper, his face pale, his eyes closed. And Lovis was kneeling beside him to bandage a wound in his neck. All the other robbers stood around gloomily, looking on. Only Matt was pacing like an angry bear, shouting and cursing.

"Oh, those dirty devils of Borka's clan and their dirty devils of robbers! Oh, those bandits! Oh, I'll crack them one by one until none of them ever stirs hand or foot again in this life! Oh, oh!"

Then he ran out of words and simply bawled without ceasing, until Lovis pointed sternly at Bumper. At last Matt realized that too much noise would not do the poor fellow any good, and he fell into unwilling silence.

Ronia knew that Matt was not the right person to talk to just now. It would be better to ask Noddle-Pete what had happened.

"People like Borka should be hanged," said Noddle-Pete. And he told her why.

Matt and his brave boys had been lying in ambush on Robbers' Walk, Noddle-Pete recounted, when by good fortune a whole mass of travelers passed: merchants with provisions and skins and a whole pile of money too. They had no way of defending themselves, so they lost all they had.

"Well, but weren't they annoyed?" Ronia asked uneasily.

"What do you think! You should have heard how they swore and carried on! And they were in a great hurry to get away. They were going to go off and complain to the sheriff, I'm sure."

Noddle-Pete chuckled, but Ronia could not find anything to chuckle about.

"And then, what do you think?" Noddle-Pete went on. "When

we had just loaded everything on our horses' backs and were turning toward home, Borka and his hangers-on came up and wanted to share in the booty. And they were shooting, the brutes! So Bumper got an arrow right in the throat. And then we shot too, of course—oh, yes, there must have been two or three of them who got the same medicine as Bumper."

Matt came up just in time to hear this. He ground his teeth. "Just wait—this is only the beginning," he said. "I'll crack each one of them in turn. Up to now I've held my peace, but now there'll be an end to all Borka robbers."

Ronia felt rage mounting within her. "But what if there's an end to all Matt's robbers too? You haven't thought of that, have you?"

"I don't intend to think of that," Matt said. "It's not going to happen."

"You don't know anything about it," said Ronia.

Then she went and sat down beside Bumper. She laid her hand on his forehead and felt how feverish he was. He opened his eyes and looked at her and gave a little smile.

"They can't finish me off the first time around," he said, but it came out rather faintly.

Ronia took his hand and held it in her own. "No, Bumper, they can't finish you off the first time around."

She sat there for a long time, holding his hand. She shed no tears, but in her heart she was weeping grievously.

Nine

BUMPER WAS FEVERISH FOR THREE DAYS. HE WAS VERY SICK AND LAY inert, but Lovis had many medical skills and cared for him like a mother with her herbs and compresses. To everyone's surprise he got up on the fourth day, weak in the legs but otherwise quite spry. The arrow had struck a neck tendon, and as the tendon healed, it contracted more and more. This made Bumper's head tip to one side, which gave him a rather melancholy appearance, although he was just as bold and merry as ever. All the robbers were glad he had survived, and they were only joking when they sometimes shouted "Skewhead!" when they wanted him for something. And Bumper was not at all distressed.

The only one who was distressed was Ronia. The hatred between

Matt and Borka made life hard for her. She had believed that their hostility would gradually die away, but instead it had flared up and grown dangerous. Every morning when Matt rode out through the Wolf's Neck with his robbers, she wondered how many of them would come back unscathed. She was not content until they were all gathered around the long table again at night. But next morning the anxiety was there again.

One day she asked her father, "Why do you and Borka have to be out for each other's blood?"

"Ask Borka," said Matt. "He shot the first arrow. Bumper can tell you that."

But Lovis too finally spoke up. "The child has more sense than you have, Matt! This can only end in bloodshed and misery, and what good will that do?"

Matt was enraged to find both Ronia and Lovis against him. "What good would it do?" he shouted. "What *good* would it do? It would get Borka out of Matt's Wood at last. Can't you understand that, you goose!"

"And does it have to be done by bloodshed, so that everyone is dead before you give in?" Ronia asked. "Is there no other way?"

Matt glowered at her. It was all very well to squabble with Lovis about it, but to have Ronia disagree with him was more than he could stand.

"You find another way then, since you're so clever! You get Borka out of Matt's Fort! Then he can settle down as peaceful as fox muck in the forest, and all his thieving hounds with him. I won't lay a hand on them."

He stopped and thought for a little, then muttered, "But if I'm not allowed to kill Borka, at least, I'll be known as a knave among robbers!"

Ronia went on meeting Birk in the woods every day. That was her consolation. But now she was no longer able to enjoy the spring carelessly, and neither was Birk.

"Even spring has been ruined for us," said Birk. "By a couple of bad-tempered old robber chieftains with no sense."

Ronia thought it was sad that Matt had turned into a bad-tempered old robber chieftain with no sense. Her Matt, her forest pine, her strength—why did it feel to her now as if Birk were the one she should turn to when there was trouble?

"If I didn't have you as a brother," she said, "I don't know . . ."

They were sitting by the lake, and all the splendor of spring was around them, but they scarcely noticed it.

Ronia was thinking. "But if I didn't have you for a brother, I might not mind that Matt wants to do away with Borka." She looked at Birk and laughed. "So it's your fault that I have so many worries!"

"I don't want you to have worries," said Birk. "But it's hard for me too."

They sat for a long time, with their troubles, but they were together, and that was a comfort.

"It's upsetting, not knowing who is alive and who is dead when evening comes," said Ronia.

"No one has died yet, though," said Birk. "But that's only because the sheriff's men have started swarming through the woods again. Matt and Borka simply don't have the chance to kill each other. They have their hands full keeping away from the soldiers."

"Yes, that's true, and it's a lucky thing," said Ronia.

Birk laughed. "Imagine the sheriff's men being useful—who would have thought it?"

"All the same, it's something to worry about," Ronia said. "And I think you and I are going to have to be worried all our lives."

They went and watched the wild horses grazing. Villain and Savage were with the herd, and Birk whistled to them. They lifted their heads and looked rather thoughtful for a moment; then they went on grazing. They obviously did not consider him worth bothering about.

"You are beasts," said Birk, "no matter how good-natured you may look at the moment."

Ronia wanted to go home. Thanks to a couple of bad-tempered old robber chieftains, it was no fun staying in the woods any more.

That day, like all other days, she and Birk separated long before the Wolf's Neck and far from all robber tracks. They knew where Matt usually came riding home and where Borka's paths ran, yet they were always worried that someone might see them together.

Ronia let Birk go ahead.

"I'll see you tomorrow," he said, and off he ran.

Ronia delayed for a time, watching the fox cubs jumping and playing. They were a joy to see, but Ronia felt no joy, and she wondered glumly if things could ever be as they had been before. Perhaps she would never again rejoice in the forest as she once had.

Then she turned toward home. When she reached the Wolf's Neck, she found Jep and Little-Snip on guard. They seemed merrier than usual.

"Hurry home and see what's happened," Jep said.

Ronia was curious. "It must be something pleasant—I can tell from your faces."

"Oh, yes, you're right there," said Little-Snip with a grin. "Go and see for yourself."

Ronia began to run. She could certainly do with something pleasant.

Soon she was outside the closed door of the stone hall and could hear Matt laughing inside, a great ringing laugh that warmed her and took away all her worry. And now she wanted to find out what made him laugh so.

She ran eagerly into the stone hall. As soon as Matt caught sight of her, he rushed forward and threw his arms around her. He lifted her high in the air and swung her around, quite carried away.

"Ronia darling," he shouted, "you were right! There need be no bloodshed. Now Borka will go to blazes faster than his first belch after breakfast, believe me!"

"How so?" asked Ronia.

Matt pointed. "Look there! Look who I've just caught with my own hands!"

The stone hall was full of excited robbers jumping around and making a noise, so at first Ronia could not see what Matt was pointing at.

"You see, Ronia darling, I have only to say to Borka, 'Are you staying or going? Do you want your snake fry back or not?' "

Then she saw Birk. There he was, lying in a corner, bound hand and foot, with blood on his forehead and desperation in his eyes, and around him Matt's robbers leaped, whooping and yelling.

"Hey there, little Borkason, when are you going home to your father?"

Ronia gave a shriek, and tears of rage spurted from her eyes.

"You can't do that!" She started to beat Matt wherever she could reach with balled fists. "You beast, you can't do that!"

Matt dropped her with a thud; there was no more laughter now. He was pale with fury.

"What's that my daughter says I can't do?" he asked menacingly.

"I'll tell you," shrieked Ronia. "You can go robbing all the money and goods and rubbish you want, but you can't rob people, because if you do I don't want to be your daughter any more!"

"Who's talking about people?" said Matt, his voice unrecognizable. "I've caught a snake fry, a louse, a little thieving hound, and I'm going to get my father's fortress cleaned out at last. Then you can be my daughter or not just as you choose."

"Beast!" shrieked Ronia.

Noddle-Pete moved between them, beginning to be frightened. Never before had he seen Matt's face so stony and terrible, and it scared him.

"That's no way to talk to your father," said Noddle-Pete, taking Ronia by the arm. But she threw him off.

"Beast!" she shrieked again.

Matt seemed not to hear her. It was as if she no longer existed for him.

"Fooloks," he said, in the same terrifying voice, "go up to Hell's Gap and send a message to Borka. Tell him I want to see him there as soon as the sun rises tomorrow morning. It would be safer for him to come, tell him that!"

Lovis stood listening in silence. She drew her eyebrows together, but said nothing. Finally she went over and looked at Birk, and when she saw the wound on his forehead she fetched her crock of healing herb juices. She was about to wash the wound when Matt bellowed, "Don't you lay a hand on the snake fry!"

"Snake fry or no," said Lovis, "this wound must be washed!"

And washed it was.

Then Matt advanced. He took hold of her and flung her across the floor. If Knott had not caught her, she would have slid straight into a bedpost.

But Lovis would never let anyone get away with that. And since Matt was not within striking distance, she dealt Knott a resounding blow. That was all the thanks he got for not letting her collide with the bedpost.

"Out, every man jack of you," screamed Lovis. "I'm sick of all of you. You never do anything but make trouble. Do you hear me, Matt? Get out of here!"

Matt gave her a black look. It would have scared anyone else, but not Lovis. She stood there, her arms folded, watching him march out of the stone hall, followed by all his robbers. But over his shoulder lay Birk, his copper hair hanging limply.

"You beast, Matt!" Ronia shrieked again, before the heavy door shut behind him.

Matt did not lie in his usual bed beside Lovis that night, and where he slept Lovis did not know.

"And I don't care, either," she said. "Now I can lie lengthwise and crosswise in this bed if I choose."

But she could not sleep. She could hear her child crying desperately, and her child would not accept any comforting. It was a night Ronia had to go through alone. She lay awake a long time, hating her father until she felt her heart contract with pain. But it is difficult to hate someone whom you have loved so much all your life, and that was why this was the heaviest of nights for Ronia.

At last she fell asleep, but she woke up as soon as light began to dawn. The sun would be rising soon, and by then she must be at Hell's Gap to see what happened there. Lovis tried to stop her, but Ronia was not to be stopped. She went, and Lovis followed her silently.

And there they stood, as they had once stood before, each on his own side of Hell's Gap, Matt and Borka with their robbers. Undis was there, too, and Ronia could hear her screams and curses a long way off. It was Matt she was cursing so fiercely that the air sizzled. But Matt was not going to be insulted for long.

"Can you make your woman be quiet, Borka?" he said. "It would be best for you to hear what I have to say."

Ronia had placed herself directly behind him so that he would not see her. She herself heard and saw more than she could bear. At Matt's side stood Birk, no longer tied hand and foot, but with a rope around his neck, and Matt was holding the rope in his hand as if he were leading a dog.

"You're a hard man, Matt," said Borka. "And a vile man. I can understand that you want me out of here. But to use my child to get what you want is vile!"

"I didn't ask what you thought about me," said Matt. "What I want to know is how soon you're going to get out."

Borka was so angry that words were choked in his throat. He stood in silence for a long time, but at last he said, "First I have to find a place where we can settle down out of danger, and that may be difficult. But if you give me back my son, you have my word that we will be gone before the summer is over."

"Good," said Matt. "Then you have my word that you will get your son back before the summer is over."

"I meant I want him now," said Borka.

"And I meant that you shan't have him," said Matt. "But we have dungeons in Matt's Fort. He will not want for a roof over his head, so let that be a comfort to you if it happens to be a rainy summer."

Ronia caught her breath. Her father had thought it out so cruelly. Borka must leave now, at once; otherwise Birk would be locked up in a dungeon until the end of summer. But he would not be able to live there that long, Ronia knew. He would die, and she would no longer have a brother.

She would not have a father she could love, either. That hurt too. She wanted to punish Matt for that, and because she could no longer be his daughter, oh, how she wanted him to suffer as she herself was suffering, and how grimly she yearned to destroy everything for him and bring all his plans to naught!

And suddenly she knew—knew what she was going to do. Once, long ago, she had done it, and in a rage that time, too, but not as beside herself as she was now. Almost as if in a fever, she took a run and flew across Hell's Gap. Matt saw her in mid-leap, and a cry burst from him, the kind of cry wild animals utter in their death agony, and the blood in his robbers turned to ice, for they had heard nothing like it before. And then they saw Ronia, his Ronia, on the other side of the abyss, with his enemy. Nothing worse could possibly have happened—and nothing so incomprehensible.

It was incomprehensible to the Borka robbers too. They stared at

Ronia as if a wild harpy had unexpectedly landed in their midst.

Borka was equally confounded, but he recovered his wits quickly. Something had happened that changed everything; he could see that. Here was Matt's wild harpy of a daughter helping him out of the jam he was in. Why she should do anything so senseless he had no idea, but he hastened to put a rope around her neck and laughed to himself as he did it.

Then he shouted to Matt, "We have dungeons underground on this side too. Your daughter will not want for a roof over her head, either, if it happens to be a rainy summer. Comfort yourself with that thought, Matt!"

But Matt was beyond all comfort. Like a wounded bear he stood there, rocking his massive body as if to subdue some unbearable torment. Ronia wept as she watched him. He had dropped the rope that held Birk prisoner, but Birk still stood there, pale and crushed, looking across Hell's Gap at Ronia.

Then Undis stepped up to her and gave her a slap. "Yes, cry! I'd do the same if I had a beast like that for a father!"

But Borka told Undis to hold her tongue. She was not to interfere, he said.

Ronia herself had called Matt a beast, yet now she wished she could comfort him for what she had done to him, that had made him suffer so terribly.

Lovis, too, wanted to help him, as always when he was in need. She was standing beside him now, but he did not even notice. He noticed nothing. Just now he was alone in the world.

Then Borka called to him. "Do you hear, Matt? Are you going to give me back my son or not?"

But Matt just stood there, rocking, and did not answer.

Then Borka shouted, "Are you going to give me back my son or not?"

Matt woke up at last. "Certainly I am," he said indifferently. "When you like."

"When I like is *now*," said Borka. "Not when summer is over, but *now*!"

Matt nodded. "When you like, as I said."

It was as if it no longer concerned him. But Borka said with a grin, "And at the same time you will get back your child. Fair exchange is no robbery—you know that, you scoundrel!"

"I have no child," said Matt.

Borka's happy grin faded. "What do you mean by that? Is this some new mischief you're brewing?"

"Come and get your son," said Matt. "But you can't give me back my child, for I have none."

"But I have," screamed Lovis in a voice that lifted the crows from the battlements. "And I want my child back, understand, Borka! Now!"

Then she fixed her eyes on Matt. "Even if that child's father has gone as crazy as they come."

Matt turned and walked away with heavy footsteps.

Ten

Matt was not to be seen in the stone hall for the next few days, nor was he at the Wolf's Neck when the children were exchanged. Lovis was there instead to receive her daughter. She was supported by Fooloks and Jep, and they had Birk with them. Borka and Undis were waiting with their robbers beyond the Wolf's Neck, and Undis, full of anger and triumph, burst out as soon as she saw Lovis. "That child-robber Matt—I can well understand he's too ashamed to show his face!"

Lovis was too proud to answer. She drew Ronia to her and was about to move away without a word. She had thought a lot about the reason her daughter had put herself in Borka's hands, but at this meeting she was beginning to see something. They were looking at each other, Ronia and Birk, as if they were alone at the Wolf's Neck and in the world. Yes, no one could help seeing that these two had a bond between them.

Undis noticed at once, and she did not like what she saw. She caught hold of Birk fiercely.

"What is there between you?"

"She is my sister," said Birk. "And she saved my life."

Ronia leaned against Lovis and cried. "Just as Birk saved mine," she muttered.

But Borka was turning scarlet with anger.

"Has my son been going behind my back and keeping company with my enemy's offspring?"

"She is my sister," said Birk again, looking at Ronia.

"Sister!" shouted Undis. "Oh, yes, we know what that will mean in a year or two!"

She seized Birk and tried to pull him away.

"Don't touch me," said Birk. "I'll go by myself, and I won't have your hands on me."

He turned and went, and there came a cry of misery from Ronia. "Birk!"

But he had gone.

When Lovis was alone with Ronia, she wanted to ask a few questions, but she had no chance.

"Don't talk to me," Ronia said.

So Lovis left her in peace, and they walked home in silence.

Noddle-Pete greeted Ronia in the stone hall as if she had been rescued from the brink of death. "I'm glad you're alive," he said. "Poor child, I've been so afraid for you!"

But Ronia went off and lay down silently on her bed, drawing the curtains around her.

"There's nothing but misery in Matt's Fort," said Noddle-Pete, shaking his head gloomily. Then he whispered to Lovis, "I've got Matt in my bedroom. But he just lies there staring and never says a word. He doesn't want to get up, and he doesn't want to eat. What will we do with him?"

"He'll come when he's hungry enough," said Lovis.

But she was worried, and on the fourth day she went to Noddle-Pete's room and spoke her mind.

"Come and eat, Matt! Stop sulking! Everyone's sitting at the table, waiting for you."

Matt came at last, glum and so thin that he was scarcely recognizable. He sat down at the table without a word and began to eat. All his robbers were silent too. It had never been so silent in the stone hall. Ronia was sitting in her usual place, but Matt did not see her. She took care not to look at him either. She only shot one sideways glance at him and saw a Matt quite unlike the father she had known until then. Yes, everything was different and horrible! She wanted to jump up and run away, not to be where Matt was, to escape and be on her own. But she sat on irresolutely, not knowing what to do with all her sorrow.

"Have you had enough, you merry clowns?" Lovis said grimly when the meal was over. She could not abide all this silence.

The robbers got up, muttering, and made off as quickly as they could to their horses, now standing idle in their stalls for the fourth day running. While their chief was doing nothing but lie in Noddle-Pete's room staring at the wall, they could not go out and rob. It was too bad, they thought, since this was a time when more travelers than usual were passing through the woods.

Matt left the stone hall without having spoken a single word and was not seen again that day.

And Ronia rushed out into the woods again. She had been there for three days, looking for Birk, but he did not come; she could not think why. What were they doing to him? Had they locked him in so he would not run off to the woods and be with her? It was hard, just waiting and knowing nothing.

She sat by the lake for a long time, and the glory of spring was all around her. But without Birk it brought her no joy. She remembered how things had been before, when she was alone and the woods were enough for her. How long ago that seemed now! Now she needed Birk to share everything with. But he did not seem to be coming today either, and when she had waited until she was tired she got up to go.

Then he came. She heard him whistling among the fir trees and rushed to him, wild with happiness. There he was! And he was lugging a big bundle with him.

"I'm moving into the forest now," he said. "I can't live in Borka's Keep any longer."

Ronia gazed at him in astonishment. "Why is that?"

"The way I am, I can't put up with nagging and hard words forever," he said. "Three days are enough for me!"

Matt's silence is worse than hard words, thought Ronia, and suddenly she knew what she would do. What was unbearable could be changed! Birk had done it, so why shouldn't she do it too?

"I'm going to leave Matt's Fort, too," she said eagerly. "I will! Yes, I will!"

"I was born in a cave," said Birk, "and I live in a cave. But can you?"

"I can live anywhere at all with you," said Ronia. "Especially in the Bear's Cave!"

There were a number of caves in the mountainsides, but none as good as the Bear's Cave. Ronia had known about it ever since she first began to wander here in the woods. Matt had shown it to her. He himself had sometimes lived there when he was a boy. In the summer. In the winter bears used to sleep there, Noddle-Pete had told him, so he had called it the Bear's Cave, and that had been its name ever since.

The Bear's Cave lay near the river, high above it, right between two rocky cliffs. It could be reached only along a ledge of rock on the mountainside, which was narrow at the beginning and felt perilous, but just outside the cave it widened to a broad platform of stone. There, high above the rushing river, you could sit and watch the morning rise in all its glory over mountains and forests. Ronia had done it often. Yes, you could live in that cave, she knew.

"I'll come to the Bear's Cave late at night," she said. "That is, if you will be there?"

"Yes, where else?" said Birk. "I will be there waiting for you."

Lovis sang the Wolf Song for Ronia that night as she had always sung it at the end of every day, whether glad or sorrowful.

But this is the last night I'll hear it, Ronia thought, and it was a hard thought. It was hard to leave her mother, but still harder no longer to be Matt's child. That was why she had to go out into the woods, even if it meant she would never hear the Wolf Song again.

And it was to be now. As soon as Lovis had fallen asleep. Ronia lay in her bed staring into the fire as she waited. Lovis was stirring restlessly in her bed, but at last she was still, and Ronia could tell from her breathing that she was asleep.

Then Ronia crept out of bed and stood for a long time gazing at her sleeping mother in the light from the fire.

My darling Lovis, she thought, perhaps we will see each other again, perhaps not.

Lovis's unbound hair was spread out over the pillow. Ronia stroked the red-brown tresses with one finger. Was it really her mother lying there looking so childlike? Tired, too, and lonely without Matt beside her in the bed. And now her child was going to leave her as well.

"Forgive me," Ronia murmured. "But I must!"

Then she stole silently out of the stone hall and collected her pack, well hidden in the costume chamber. It was so heavy that she could scarcely carry it, and when she reached the Wolf's Neck, she flung the bundle right at the feet of Tapper and Torm, who were on guard that night. Not that Matt cared about posting guards any more, but Noddle-Pete did it with great enthusiasm in his stead.

Tapper stared at Ronia. "Where in the name of all wild harpies are you off to in the middle of the night?"

"I'm moving into the forest now," said Ronia. "You must tell Lovis."

"Why don't you tell her yourself?" asked Tapper.

"Well, because she wouldn't let me go! And I don't want to be stopped."

"What do you think your father will say then?" asked Torm.

"My father," Ronia said thoughtfully. "Have I got a father?"

She gave them her hand in farewell. "Give everyone my love! Don't forget Noddle-Pete! And remember me sometimes when you're dancing and singing your songs."

This was more than Tapper and Torm could bear. Tears sprang into their eyes, and Ronia cried a little too.

"I think this is the end of dancing in Matt's Fort," said Tapper sorrowfully.

Ronia picked up her bundle and threw it over her shoulder. "Tell Lovis that she must not grieve and worry too much. I'll be in the woods if she wants to find me."

"And what are we to say to Matt?" asked Torm.

"Nothing," Ronia said with a sigh.

Then she went. Tapper and Torm stood watching silently until she vanished around the bend of the path.

Now it was night, and the moon was high in the sky. Ronia stopped at the lake to rest, sat down on a stone, and felt how still everything was in her forest. She listened but could hear nothing but silence. The woods in the spring night felt full of secrets, full of magic and other strange and ancient things. There were dangers there, too, but Ronia was not afraid.

If only the wild harpies keep away, I'm as safe as in Matt's Fort, she thought. The forest is my home as it has always been, and even more so now, when I have no other home.

The lake lay there, very black, but across the water ran a narrow beam of moonlight. It was beautiful, and Ronia's heart lightened as she saw it. How strange it was that you could be happy and sad at the same time! She was sad for Matt's sake, and for Lovis, but happy about all the magic, lovely, silent treasures of the spring night about her. And it was here in the woods that she would be living from now on. With Birk. Now she remembered he was waiting for her in the Bear's Cave—why was she sitting here, thinking?

She got up and lifted her bundle. It was a long way to the cave, and there was no path for her to follow, but she knew exactly how to reach it. In the same way as the animals knew it, and as all the rumphobs and murktrolls and gray dwarfs of the forest knew it. So she walked calmly through the moonlit woods, between the pines and fir trees, over moss and blueberry twigs, past marshland scented with bog myrtle, and past black, bottomless pools. She climbed over mossy fallen trees and waded through rippling brooks; straight through the woods she walked, heading unerringly for the Bear's Cave.

She saw the murktrolls dancing in the moonlight on a rocky outcrop. They did it only on moonlit nights, Noddle-Pete had told her, and she stopped for a while to watch them without their noticing. It was a strange dance they were performing, swaying around very quietly and clumsily, and humming to themselves all the while. Noddle-Pete had told her this was their spring song and had tried to hum it to her in the manner of trolls, but it was not very much like what she now heard—such an ancient, sorrowful sound.

When she thought of Noddle-Pete, she had to think of Matt and Lovis too, and the thought hurt her.

But she forgot it when at last she reached the cave and saw the fire—yes, Birk had lit a fire on the rocky shelf outside the cave so they would not freeze in the cold spring night. It flickered and flared so she could see it at a distance, and she remembered what Matt used to say: "Where there is a home, there is a fire!"

And where there is a fire, there can also be a home, Ronia thought. There was going to be a home in the Bear's Cave!

And there sat Birk, quite at peace beside the fire, eating grilled steak. He speared a piece of meat on a stick and handed it to her.

"I've been waiting a long time," he said. "Now eat—before you sing the Wolf Song!"

Eleven

RONIA TRIED TO SING THE WOLF SONG FOR BIRK AS SOON AS THEY were lying on their fir-branch beds. But when she remembered how Lovis had sung it for her and Matt when everything was still as it used to be in Matt's Fort, she felt such a tug of yearning in her breast that she could not go on.

And Birk was already falling asleep. All day while he waited for her he had worked to clean up the cave after the bear which had recently finished its winter sleep there. Then he had dragged up from the woods kindling for the fire and branches to sleep on. He had had a strenuous day and was soon asleep.

Ronia lay awake. It was dark in the cave, and cold, but she was not freezing. Birk had lent her a goatskin to spread over the fir branches, and she had brought her squirrelskin coverlet with her from her bed at home. It was soft and warm to wrap herself in. There was no need for her to lie awake because of the cold, but still sleep would not come.

For a long time she lay there, not feeling as happy as she wished, but through the cave opening she could see the light, cool sky of spring and she could hear the river rushing deep down in its gully, and that helped.

It's the same sky over Matt's Fort, she thought. And the same river rushing by that I can hear at home.

And then she slept.

Both of them woke up when the sun rose over the ridge on the other side of the river. Flaming red, it appeared from the morning mist and flared like a torch over the forest near and far.

"I'm blue with cold," said Birk, "but dawn is the coldest hour—then it gets warmer bit by bit. Isn't it a comfort to know that?"

"A fire would be still more comfort," said Ronia, whose teeth were chattering too. Birk poked life into the embers, and they sat beside their fire, eating their bread and drinking what was left of the goat's milk that Ronia had brought.

When the last mouthful was gone, Ronia said, "From now on we'll be drinking spring water and nothing else."

"It won't make us fat," said Birk, "but we won't die of it either."

They looked at each other and laughed. Their life in the Bear's Cave would be hard, they knew, but it did not affect their spirits. Ronia did not even remember that she had been unhappy in the night. Now they were well-fed and warm, the morning was bright, and they were as free as birds. It was as if they had not realized it until this moment. Everything that had been so heavy and hard in recent days was now behind them; they were going to forget it; they never wanted to think of it again.

"Ronia," said Birk, "do you realize that *we are free*?" He threw back his head and roared with laughter at the very thought.

"Yes, and this is our kingdom," said Ronia. "No one can take it away from us or drive us out."

They went on sitting by their fire as the sun rose. The river rushed below them, and all around them the whole forest had awakened. The treetops stirred quietly in the morning breeze, the cuckoos called, a woodpecker hammered at a tree trunk somewhere nearby, and on the other side of the river an elk family appeared at the edge of the woods. And the two of them sat there, feeling as if they ruled over everything—river and wood and all the living things in them.

"Cover your ears—my spring yell is coming," said Ronia.

And she gave a yell that echoed among the mountains.

"There's one thing I hope more than anything else," said Birk. "To be able to fetch my crossbow before you bring the wild harpies down on us with your yelling."

"Fetch . . . where from?" Ronia asked. "From Borka's Keep?"

"No, in the woods outside it," said Birk. "I couldn't bring everything with me at once, so I made myself a hiding place in a hollow tree, and I've got all kinds of bits and pieces there that I want to bring here."

"Matt didn't want me to have a crossbow yet," said Ronia. "But I can cut myself an ordinary bow if I can borrow your knife."

"Yes, if you take care of it. It's the most precious thing we have, remember that. Without a knife we can't manage in the woods."

"There are other things we can't manage without," said Ronia. "Buckets to carry the water in—have you thought of that?"

Birk laughed. "I certainly have thought. But thoughts carry no water."

"That's why it's a good thing that I know where to get one," said Ronia.

"Where?"

"In Lovis's healing spring, in the woods below the Wolf's Neck. She sent Bumper there yesterday for the healing water Noddle-Pete had to take for his stomach. But Bumper got a pair of wild harpies after him and came home without the buckets. He'll have to get them today—Lovis will see to that, believe me! But if I hurry I may get there before him."

And they both hurried off. They ran, light-footed, all the long way across the woods and got the things they needed. It was some time before they were back at the cave, Ronia with buckets, Birk with his crossbow and other things from his hiding place. He lined them all up on the slab outside the cave to show Ronia what he had. An ax, a whetstone, a small cooking pot, fishing gear, snares for catching birds, arrows for his crossbow, a short spear—all necessary things for people who were going to live in the woods.

"Yes, I see you know what we woodsmen have to do," said Ronia. "Get our own food and defend ourselves against harpies and beasts of prey."

"I know that well enough," said Birk. "Of course we will—"

He got no further, for Ronia had grabbed at his arm and was whispering fearfully, "Quiet! There's someone inside the cave."

They held their breath and listened. Yes, there was someone in their cave, someone who had taken care to steal in while they were away. Birk picked up his spear, and they stood waiting in silence. They could hear someone moving around inside, and it was uncanny not knowing who was there. In fact, there seemed to be more than one. Perhaps the whole cave was full of harpies, lying in wait, ready to come rushing out at any moment and dig their claws into them.

Finally they could not bear to listen and wait any longer.

"Come out, harpies!" shouted Birk. "If you want to meet the sharpest spear in these woods!"

But no one came out. Instead they heard an angry hissing from inside the cave. "People here in Gray Dwarfs' Woods! Gray dwarfs all, bite and strike!"

That made Ronia blaze with anger. "Out with you, gray dwarfs," she shouted. "Be off with you, at once! Otherwise I'll come and pull your hair out!"

And out of the cave swarmed the gray dwarfs, hissing and spitting at Ronia. But she spat back at them, and Birk showed them his spear. At that they were in a hurry to get down the mountainside. They crawled and clambered down the steep cliff, trying to reach the river. Some of them lost their grip and fell, squealing with rage, into the waterfalls, so that whole clumps of gray dwarfs went sailing down the river. But they managed to struggle ashore at last.

"They're good swimmers, those little beasts," Ronia said.

"And good bread eaters, too," said Birk, when they went into the cave and saw that the gray dwarfs had eaten a whole loaf from their stores.

They had had no time to do worse, but the fact that they had been there was enough.

"This is not at all good," said Ronia. "The whole forest will be hissing and spitting with their chatter, and soon every last harpy will know where we are."

But you were not allowed to be afraid in Matt's Forest. Ronia had been hearing that since she was small. And it was stupid to live in dread of something that had not happened, both she and Birk thought, so they calmly arranged their food supplies and weapons and tools in the cave. Then they got water from a spring in the forest and laid a net in the river to catch fish. They dragged home flat stones from the river's edge and made themselves a hearth on their platform, and they searched far and wide to find juniper wood for Ronia's bow. As they walked, they saw the wild horses grazing in the usual glade and tried to approach Villain and Savage, speaking gently to them, but with no result. Neither Villain nor Savage understood kindness; they made off, running lightly, to graze somewhere else, where they could be left in peace.

For the rest of the day Ronia sat outside the cave, cutting her bow and two arrows for it. She gave up a length of her leather rope as a bowstring. Then she practiced shooting, long and happily, until at last she had lost both her arrows. She hunted for them until dusk began to fall and she had to give up. But it did not bother her much.

"I'll cut some new ones tomorrow."

"And you take care of the knife," said Birk.

"Yes, I know it's the most precious thing we have. The knife and the ax!"

Suddenly they noticed that it was already night and that they were hungry. The day had flown past, and they had been busy all the time. They had walked and run and carried and dragged and gotten things organized and had no time to feel hungry. But now they treated themselves to a feast of bread and sheep's cheese and mutton and washed it down with clear spring water, just as Ronia had predicted.

The night was never dark at this time of year, but their tired bodies could feel that the day was over and that they wanted to sleep.

In the darkness of the cave Ronia sang the Wolf's Song for Birk, and this time it went better. All the same, it made her sad again, and she asked Birk, "Do you think they're thinking about us in Matt's Fort? Our parents, I mean!"

"It would be odd if they didn't."

Ronia swallowed before she could speak again. "Will they be sorry, do you think?"

Birk thought a bit. "It will be different. Undis will be sorry, but she'll be even more angry, I think. Borka will be angry too, but more sad at the same time."

"Lovis will be sorry—I know that," said Ronia.

"What about Matt?" asked Birk.

Ronia was silent for a long time, then she said, "I should think he's quite pleased. That I've gone, so that he can forget me."

And she tried to believe it, but in her heart she knew that it was not true.

That night she dreamed that Matt was sitting alone in the middle of a dark, black wood, crying until there was a pool at his feet. And deep down in the pool she herself sat, small again, playing with pinecones and pebbles he had given her.

Twelve

EARLY NEXT MORNING THEY WENT DOWN TO THE RIVER TO SEE IF they had caught any fish in the net. "Fish must be hauled in before the cuckoo calls," Ronia said.

She skipped merrily down the path ahead of Birk. It was a narrow little path, winding steeply down the mountainside through a grove of young birches. Ronia could smell the scent of the fresh young birch leaves, the scent of spring, and it made her happy, so she skipped.

Behind her came Birk, not yet quite awake.

"If there are any fish to haul in, yes. I suppose you think the net will be full?"

"There are salmon in this river," said Ronia. "It would be odd if not a single one had popped into our net."

"And it would be odd if you, my sister, didn't skip headfirst into the river."

"This is my spring skipping," Ronia said.

Birk laughed. "Spring skipping, yes, this path was just made for it. Who do you think trod it down to begin with?"

"Matt, perhaps," said Ronia. "When he was staying in the Bear's Cave. He likes salmon—he always has."

Then she stopped. She did not want to think about what Matt liked or didn't like. She remembered what she had dreamed the night before, and she wanted to forget that too. But the thought kept on coming back like the most stubborn gadfly and would not leave her alone. Until she saw the salmon flapping and splashing in their net! It was a fine, big salmon which would give them food for many days, and as Birk took it out of the net, he said delightedly, "Well, you're not going to die of hunger, sister mine—I promise you that."

"Until the winter," said Ronia.

But it was a long time until winter—what did she care about that now? She would have nothing more to do with any plaguing thoughts.

They returned to the cave with the salmon hanging from a stick and a fallen birch dragging behind them. It was attached to their belts by the leather rope, and they toiled painfully up the path with it, like a pair of draft horses towing timber. They needed the wood, from which they planned to make bowls and other useful items.

Birk had trimmed the birch, but the ax had skidded as he did it, and now he was bleeding from a wound in one foot. There was a trail of blood behind him on the path, but that did not bother him.

"It's nothing to worry about. The wound has to bleed until it's finished."

"Don't be so cocky," said Ronia. "A killer bear might come and follow your trail, wondering where there was more of that lovely blood."

Birk laughed. "Then I'd show it to him with a spear in my hand."

"Lovis," Ronia said thoughtfully, "usually puts on dried moss when there is bleeding. I think I'd better get ourselves a supply. Who knows when you're planning to cut yourself in the leg again?"

And so she carried home a whole armload of moss from the forest and left it to dry in the sun. Birk gave her grilled salmon when she got home. And it was not the last time. For a long time they did nothing but eat salmon and work on their wooden bowls. Cutting into the wood was not difficult; they were successful with that, and they did not cut themselves. Soon they had five splendid blocks of wood just waiting to be hollowed out into bowls. That was the number they needed, they had decided.

But by the third day Ronia was asking, "Birk, which do you think is worse—grilled salmon or blisters on your hands?"

Birk said he could not answer because one was as bad as the other.

"But I know one thing. We should have had some kind of chisel. With only a knife this is sheer slavery."

But they had no other tools, and they took turns hacking and scratching until at last they had something resembling a bowl.

"I'll never make any more of these in my life," said Birk. "Now I'm just going to sharpen the knife one more time. Hand it over!"

"The knife?" Ronia said. "You've got it yourself."

Birk shook his head. "No, you had it last. Hand it over!"

"I have no knife," said Ronia. "Didn't you hear what I said?"

"What have you done with it then?"

Ronia was getting angry. "What have *you* done with it? You were the one who had it last!"

"That's a lie," Birk said.

In resentful silence they hunted for the knife, everywhere, inside the cave and outside on the platform. And in the cave again and outside again. But it was not there.

Birk looked coldly at Ronia. "I thought I told you that without the knife we can't manage in the woods."

"Then you should have taken better care of it," said Ronia. "In any case you're a mean devil, blaming other people when you yourself have caused the trouble."

Birk turned pale with rage. "I see, so you're back again, robber's daughter! You're your old self, I see. And I'm supposed to live with you!"

"You needn't worry, Borka robber," said Ronia. "You can live with your knife! If you can find it."

She left him, tears of fury in her eyes. She would go off into the forest now, to avoid him. She never wanted to see him again, to speak one more word to him!

Birk watched her leave. That annoyed him even more, and he shouted after her, "May the harpies take you! You'll be quite at home with them!"

He saw the moss lying there, making a mess. That had been Ronia's stupid idea, and in his anger he kicked it away.

Under the moss lay the knife. Birk stared at it for a long time before he picked it up. They had searched through the moss so carefully. How could the knife be there now, and whose fault was it that it was there?

The moss was Ronia's fault in any case; that much he knew. Anyway, she was unfair and stupid and unbearable. Otherwise he would have rushed after her and told her that the knife had been found, but she might as well stay in the woods until she was tired and became reasonable again.

He whetted the knife until it was sharp. Then he sat down holding it and felt how well it lay in his hand. It was a fine knife, and it was no longer missing.

What was missing was his anger. It had left him while he was working with the knife. So he ought to be quite content now—after all, he had his knife. But Ronia had gone. Was that why he felt this odd gnawing in his chest?

You can live with your knife! That was what she had said. Now he was getting angry again. Where would *she* live? Not that it had anything to do with him; she could go and chase herself wherever she liked. But if she did not come back, and quickly, she had better watch out for herself. She would find the Bear's Cave ruthlessly closed against her! He wished he could have let her know that. But he had no intention of running through the forest looking for her to tell her. She would be coming back soon enough, begging and pleading and wanting to come in, and then he would say, "You should have come before! Now it's too late."

He said it aloud to hear how it sounded, and he shivered. What a thing to say to someone who was supposed to be his sister! But it had been her own choice. He had not driven her out.

He ate a little salmon while he waited. Salmon was marvelous the first three or four times you ate it, but now, after the tenth time, the fragments swelled in his mouth and it was difficult to get them down.

All the same, it was food. What did someone wandering in the woods eat? What was Ronia eating? There must be roots and green leaves, if she could find any, but that was not his business either. She could walk until she withered away, since that was obviously what she wanted. Since she still had not come back.

The hours passed. The place was oddly empty without Ronia. He could not think of anything to do when she was not there. And the gnawing in his chest was getting worse and worse.

He watched the dusk move in over the river, and it reminded him of that time, long ago, when he had fought against the Unearthly Ones for Ronia. He had never talked to her about it afterward, and she probably did not know that she was a person who could be lured away by their powers. How unfair she had been to him that time! She had bitten his cheek, too, and he still had a little scar from the bite. But he had liked her anyway—yes, even the first time he saw her he'd liked her. Of course, she did not know that; he had not told her that either. And now it was too late. From now on he was going to be living alone in the cave. With his knife . . . How could she say something so cruel? He would gladly fling the knife in the river if only he could have Ronia back again; he knew that now.

There was often a mist over the river in the evening; that was nothing to worry about. But who could be certain, he thought, that on this particular evening it might not rise and spread right through the woods? Then the Unearthly Ones might come out of their murky depths again. Who would protect Ronia against their wiles this time? Of course, it was no longer his business, but no matter how things stood, this could not go on any longer. He must go into the forest, he must find Ronia.

He ran until he was breathless. He looked for her everywhere on the paths and in the places where he thought she might be. He called her name until he was afraid of his own voice and afraid of attracting inquisitive, wicked harpies.

May the harpies take you, he had called after her, he remembered now with shame. Perhaps that was just what they had done, too, since she was nowhere to be found. Or what if she had gone back to Matt's Fort? Perhaps she was now kneeling before Matt, begging and pleading to be allowed to come home and be his child again. She would never beg and plead to be allowed back into the Bear's Cave—no, it was Matt she longed for, he could see that now, although she had not wanted Birk to know. So now she was probably happy, now she had someone to blame, so that she could leave the Bear's Cave and the person who was supposed to be her brother!

It was no use searching any longer. He was giving up now. He would have to go home to his cave and the loneliness there, no matter how bitter it might be.

The spring evening was as beautiful as a miracle, but Birk did not notice. He did not smell the evening scents or hear the birdsong; he did not see the grass and flowers on the ground; he could only feel the pain of his regret.

Then, far away, he heard a horse neighing in deadly fear. He ran toward the sound and heard the screams grow more and more desperate as he approached. Then he saw the horse in a little glade among the pines. It was a mare, and she was bleeding heavily from an open wound in her flank. She was afraid of Birk—that was obvious—but she did not run away; she only neighed still more fearfully, as if asking for help and protection in her need.

"Poor thing," said Birk. "Who has been treating you so badly?"

At the same moment he saw Ronia. She came rushing toward them between the pines, her face wet with tears.

"Did you see the bear?" she shouted. "Oh, Birk, he took her foal, he killed it!"

She was weeping desperately, but Birk could feel only the wildest joy. Ronia was alive. The bear had not killed her, and neither Matt nor any harpies had taken her from him. What joy!

But Ronia was standing beside the mare, looking at the blood running from her. She seemed to hear Lovis's voice in her ear and knew what to do.

She called to Birk. "Hurry! Get the moss—otherwise she'll lose all her blood!"

"But what about you? You can't stay here with a killer bear around."

"Run!" shouted Ronia. "I must stay with the mare, she needs comfort—and moss. But go quickly!"

And Birk ran. While he was gone, Ronia stood holding the mare's head between her hands. She murmured comforting words as best she could, and the mare stood still, as if listening. She was no longer neighing; perhaps she no longer had the energy. From time to time a violent shudder went through her body. It was a terrible wound that the bear had opened up. Poor mare, she had tried to protect her foal, but now he was dead. And perhaps she could feel the life dripping slowly and inevitably away from herself too. It was twilight now. Night would soon fall, and this mare would never see another morning unless Birk got back before it was too late.

But he came, his arms full of moss, and Ronia had never seen a more precious sight. She would tell him that sometime, but not now. Now they must hurry.

They helped each other to press the moss into the wound and saw how quickly it was soaked with blood. Then they put on more moss and bound it fast with the leather ropes crisscrossing the mare's flank. She stood still, letting them work, as if she understood what they were doing. But from behind the nearest pine a rumphob stuck his head out unexpectedly, and he did not understand.

"Woffor are they doing that?" he said darkly.

But Ronia and Birk were glad to see him, because now they knew that the bear had gone. Bears and wolves shunned anything to do with the shadow folk. No rumphobs or murktrolls, no harpies or gray dwarfs had to fear beasts of prey. The first smell of the shadow folk was enough to send a bear shuffling silently off into the depths of the forest.

"That foal, see," said the rumphob. "Not any more! Finish! Not running at all!"

"We know that," Ronia said sadly.

They stayed with the mare all night. It was a night of vigil and a night of cold, but it did them no harm. They sat side by side under a thick pine and talked of many things, but never of their quarrel. It was as if they had forgotten it. Ronia tried to tell Birk how she had seen the bear killing the foal, but stopped. It was too hard.

"Those are the kind of things that happen in Matt's Wood and in every wood," said Birk.

In the middle of the night they changed the moss on the wound. Then they slept for a time and woke up just as day was dawning.

"Look, it's stopped bleeding," said Ronia. "The moss is dry!"

They began to walk home toward the cave, leading the mare as she could not be left alone. It was painful and difficult for her to walk, but she followed them willingly.

"She can't climb the rocks even when she's well again," said Birk. "Where shall we put her?"

Below the cave, hidden among pines and birches, rose the spring that gave them water. They led the mare to it.

"Drink and you'll get new blood," Ronia said.

The mare drank deep and long. Afterward Birk tied her to a tree.

"She can stay here until the wound has healed. And no bears will come here, I can promise you."

Ronia stroked the mare. "Don't grieve so much," she said. "You'll have a new foal next year."

Then she saw that milk was dripping from the mare's udder.

"The little foal should have had that milk," said Ronia, "but you can give it to us instead."

She got the wooden bowl from the cave—its moment had come now. And she milked the mare until the bowl was full. It was a relief for the mare to have her tight udder emptied, and Birk was glad of the milk.

"We have a domestic animal!" he said. "And we must give her a name. What do you think she should be called?"

Ronia did not have to think long. "I think she should be called Lia. Matt had a mare when he was little, and that was her name."

And they agreed that it was a good name for a mare. A mare which was not going to die. Lia would live; they could see that now.

They cut grass and brought it to her, and she ate hungrily. Then they began to feel their own hunger; they must go back to the cave and get something to satisfy it. But Lia turned her head and watched them anxiously when they left her.

"Don't be frightened," said Ronia. "We'll be back soon. And thank you for the milk you gave us!"

It was wonderful to be drinking milk again, fresh and cooled in the cold spring water, and they sat on the platform outside the cave and ate their bread and drank their milk and saw the sun rise for a new day.

"It was a pity the knife was lost," Ronia said.

Then at last Birk took out the knife and placed it in her hand. "And it was a good thing that it came back again. It was only under the moss, waiting, while we were squabbling with each other."

Ronia sat quietly for a long time. Then she said, "Do you know what I've been thinking? I've been thinking how easily everything can be ruined, quite unnecessarily."

"From now on we are going to watch out for those unnecessary things," said Birk. "But do you know what I've been thinking? I've been thinking you're worth more than a thousand knives!"

Ronia looked at him and laughed. "Now you certainly are as crazy as they come!" That was what Lovis sometimes said to Matt.

Thirteen

THE DAYS PASSED, SPRING TURNED TO SUMMER, THE WEATHER WAS warm. And the rain came. For days and nights it poured down over the forest, which drank itself fresh and green as never before. And when the rain moved on and the sun came back again, the forest steamed in the summer heat until Ronia had to ask Birk if he thought there was so much sweet scent in any other forest on earth. He said he didn't think there was.

Lia's wound had long since healed. They had let her go, and now she was living with the wild horses again, but they were still allowed to milk her. In the evening her herd usually stopped near the cave, and every evening Ronia and Birk went out into the woods and called her. She answered with a neigh to show them where she was, because she wanted to be milked.

The others in the herd soon stopped being frightened of the human children too. Sometimes they came close and looked on curiously while Lia was being milked, for they had never seen such a thing before. Villain and Savage came often, and so close that Lia laid back her ears and snapped at them. But that did not trouble them. They went on mischievously bumping each other, tossing and leaping mightily; they were young and wanted to play. And then in a moment they would set off at a gallop and disappear in the woods.

But the very next evening they were there again. They could be talked to now, and at last they could even be patted. Ronia and Birk went on patting them busily, and they actually seemed to like it. All the same, there was always a gentle mischief in their eyes, as if they were thinking, You can't fool us!

But one evening Ronia said, "I've said I'm going to ride, and I am!"

It was Birk's turn to do the milking, and Villain and Savage were standing close by, looking on.

"Did you hear what I said?"

She was speaking to Villain, and suddenly she had clutched his mane and sprung onto his back. He threw her off, but not as easily as before. She was ready now and knew what to expect. He had to work hard to get rid of her, but he managed it at last, and she plumped into the brook with a shriek of rage. She got up again, relatively unscathed, and rubbed her sore elbows.

"You are and will remain a villain," she said, "but I'll be back! You'll see!"

And she was. Every evening after milking they both tried, she and Birk, to teach Villain and Savage better manners. But no teaching worked with those wicked beasts, and when Ronia had been thrown off enough, she said, "Now there is not one bit of my body that doesn't hurt." She gave Villain a slap. "And it's your fault, you dirty devil!"

But Villain stood there calmly, looking very satisfied with himself.

She saw Birk still struggling with Savage. Savage was as difficult as Villain, but Birk was strong and stayed on his back—yes, he actually stayed on until Savage grew tired and gave up.

"Look, Ronia," Birk shouted, "he's standing still!"

Savage whinnied uneasily, but he stood still, and Birk patted him and praised him immoderately until at last Ronia had to speak out.

"In his heart he's still a dirty devil—you know that!"

It annoyed her that Birk had succeeded with Savage when she could not manage Villain. And it annoyed her still more that after that, in the evenings, Birk left her to milk alone while he rode around her in tight circles on Savage's back as she knelt to milk. Just to show what a horseman he was.

"Bruises or no," Ronia said at last, "you wait till I've finished milking, and you'll see some riding!"

And he did. Villain did not know what had happened when he suddenly found Ronia on his back again. He did not like it and set off at full speed to throw her off, and he was both frightened and resentful when he realized that it did no good. No, this time he was not going to throw her, Ronia had decided. She kept a firm grip on his mane, she gripped with her knees, and she sat tight. Then he flew off straight into the woods, the fir and pine branches whining around her ears. He was bolting, and she shrieked in terror, "Help! Help!"

But Villain had completely lost his head. He tore along as if he were ready to burst, and Ronia was expecting at any moment to tumble off and break her neck.

Then Birk came chasing after her on Savage, and that horse was a runner like no other. Soon Savage had caught up with Villain and passed him. Then Birk pulled Savage up sharply. Villain, galloping at full speed after him, had to stop dead, and Ronia flew halfway over his head. But she clung on, she got back into her seat, and Villain stood there, disappointed, having run himself out. The foam dripped from him, and he was shuddering, but Ronia patted him and praised him to the skies for his running, which calmed him down.

"You should really be getting it in the neck," she said. "It's a miracle that I'm still alive!"

"It's a bigger miracle that we're riding," said Birk. "Look, at last both these two wicked beasts know what they're supposed to do and who decides!"

They rode back to Lia at the calmest of trots, got their milk, and left Villain and Savage to their games. And then Ronia and Birk went home to their cave.

"Birk," she said, "have you noticed that Lia is giving less milk?"

"Yes, she will have a new foal on the way now," said Birk. "And soon she'll dry up altogether."

"Then it will be spring water for us again," Ronia said, "and we'll soon be having to manage without bread too."

The flour Ronia had brought from home was finished. They had baked the last hard loaves on the heated stones of the hearth. There was still some bread left in the cave, but soon that would be gone. They would not starve; there were many little lakes in the forest, full of fish, and there were plenty of forest birds, too. They could always snare themselves a grouse if hunger threatened. Ronia picked herbs and the kind of green leaves that could be eaten, as Lovis had taught her to do. And by now the wild strawberries were ripe, lying red and plentiful about the fallen trees. Soon the blueberries would be ripe too.

"No, we won't starve," said Ronia. "But I'm not going to enjoy the first day without bread or milk!"

And that day came sooner than they had expected. Lia responded loyally when they called her in the evening, but Ronia could see that she no longer liked to be milked. Finally Ronia could not get more than a few drops out of her, and Lia showed her clearly that she had had enough.

Then Ronia took Lia's head between her hands and looked into her eyes.

"I want to thank you, Lia, for these past days. Next summer you will have another foal—do you know that? And then you will have milk again. But that is for your foal, not for us."

Ronia stroked the mare, persuading herself that Lia understood every word, and she told Birk, "You must thank her too!"

And Birk did. They stayed with the mare a long time, and when they left her she followed them a little way through the light summer night. It was almost as if she understood that it was over now, this strange time she had been living through, which was not at all like the rest of her life as a wild horse. The little human beings who had made strange things happen were now going away from her, and she stood there for a time, watching them until they disappeared among the spruce trees. Then she turned back to her herd.

They saw her sometimes in the evenings when they came out to ride, and if they called her name she whinnied in answer, but she never left the herd to come to them. She was a wild horse and she would never be a domestic animal, after all.

But Villain and Savage came running eagerly as soon as they saw Ronia and Birk. There was nothing they enjoyed more nowadays than racing each other, each with a rider on his back. And Ronia and Birk got enormous pleasure from their long rides through the forest.

But one evening they were chased by a wild harpy. The horses went crazy with terror and became impossible to handle or guide. And all Ronia and Birk could do was to throw themselves off and let the horses run. Without riders the horses had nothing to fear—it was human beings that the wild harpies hated and wanted to get at, not the beasts of the forest.

But Ronia and Birk were in danger now. Terrified, they rushed off in opposite directions. The harpy could not catch them both, but they knew that in her stupidity she would try, and that was what saved them. While she was chasing Birk, Ronia managed to hide. It was worse for Birk, but when the harpy tried furiously to see where Ronia had gone to and forgot Birk for one short moment, he crawled quickly down between two great boulders and sat there for a long time, expecting the harpy to find him again at any moment.

But with harpies, what they couldn't see did not exist. There was no human being there now whose eyes she could claw out, and she flew back to the mountains in a rage to let all her fierce sisters know about it.

Birk watched her go, and when he was certain that she would not come back, he called Ronia. Ronia crept out of her hiding place under a spruce and they danced around, rejoicing over their safety. What luck, neither of them had been clawed to death by wild harpies or carried up to the caves in the mountains to a life in captivity!

"You shouldn't be frightened in Matt's Forest," said Ronia. "But with wild harpies flapping around your ears it's difficult not to be."

There was no sign of Villain and Savage, so they now had to walk the long way home to the Bear's Cave.

"But I could walk all night as long as I don't see a wild harpy," said Birk.

And they walked through the woods, holding hands and talking happily, in high spirits after all that fear. Dusk was falling now; it was a beautiful summer evening, and they talked about the wonderful time they could have, even though there were wild harpies. How lovely it was to live in the freedom of the forest, by night or by day, under the sun, moon, and stars and through the slow passage of the seasons, in springtime, which was just over now, in summertime, which had begun, and in the autumn, which would be coming soon.

"But in winter . . ." said Ronia, and then she stopped.

They saw rumphobs and murktrolls and gray dwarfs chattering and peeping out curiously, now here, now there, from behind tree trunks and boulders.

"Shadow folk," said Ronia. "They go on living quite cheerfully in wintertime too."

Then she was silent again.

"Sister mine, it's summer now," said Birk, and Ronia could feel that it was.

"I'll carry this summer around in my memory as long as I live," she said.

Birk looked around in the twilight woods, and a strange mood came upon him; he did not know why. He did not understand that what he was feeling, almost like pain, was only the beauty and peace of the summer evening, nothing more.

"This summer," he said, looking at Ronia. "Yes, I shall carry this summer with me till the end of my life—I know that."

So they came home to the Bear's Cave. And on the platform outside sat Little-Snip, waiting for them.

Fourteen

LITTLE-SNIP WAS SITTING THERE, FLAT-NOSED AND TOUSLE-HAIRED and bearded, as Ronia had always known him. But now she felt she had never seen a finer sight, and she threw herself at him with a shriek.

"Little-Snip . . . oh, is it you . . . you . . . you've come!"

She was so happy it made her stammer.

"Nice view here," said Little-Snip. "You can see the river and the woods, can't you?"

Ronia laughed. "Yes, you can see the river and the woods! Is that why you're here?"

"No, no, Lovis sent me with some bread," said Little-Snip. He opened his leather bag and took out five big, round loaves.

Then Ronia screamed, "Birk, did you see? Bread! We've got bread!"

She seized a loaf and held it up, she breathed in the fragrance, and tears came to her eyes.

"Lovis's bread! I'd forgotten there was anything so wonderful."

And she broke off great chunks and stuffed them in her mouth. She wanted to give Birk some too, but he stood darkly by, and without a word, without taking any bread, he went off into the cave.

"Yes, Lovis worked out that you must be out of bread about now," said Little-Snip.

Ronia chewed, tasting the bread like a blessing in her mouth, and it made her miss Lovis. But now she had to ask Little-Snip, "How did Lovis know that I was in the Bear's Cave?"

Little-Snip sniffed. "Do you think your mother's stupid? Where else would you be?"

He looked at her thoughtfully. There she sat, their Ronia, their lovely little Ronia, stuffing bread into herself as if it were all she wanted in life. Now he must get on with what he had really come for. Lovis had told him he had to be cunning, and he was worried. For Little-Snip was not especially cunning.

"Look, Ronia," he said cautiously, "won't you come home soon?"

There was a clattering inside the cave. Someone was listening and wanted Ronia to know it.

But Ronia was thinking only of Little-Snip just now. There was so much she wanted to ask him, so much she longed to know. He was sitting beside her, but when she wanted to go on with her questions she found she could not look at him. Instead, she sat looking out over the river and the trees.

Then she asked, so quietly that Little-Snip could scarcely hear her, "How are things in Matt's Fort nowadays?"

And Little-Snip told her the truth. "It's melancholy in Matt's Fort nowadays. Come home, Ronia!"

Ronia looked out over the river and the trees again. "Did Lovis send you to say that?"

Little-Snip nodded. "Yes! It's too difficult without you, Ronia. Everyone is waiting for you to come home."

Ronia, still looking out over the river and the trees, asked quietly, "Matt? Is he waiting for me to come home too?"

Little-Snip swore. "That beast of Satan! Who knows what he's thinking and what he's waiting for!"

There was a short silence, and then Ronia asked, "Does he ever talk about me?"

Little-Snip wriggled. It was now that he was supposed to be cunning, so he remained silent.

"Tell me the truth," said Ronia. "Does he ever mention my name?"

"No," said Little-Snip unwillingly. "And no one else is allowed to either, not in his hearing."

Devil take it, now he had said what Lovis wanted him to keep quiet about! Oh, yes, he was cunning all right!

He looked pleadingly at Ronia. "But everything will be all right if only you'll come home!"

Ronia shook her head. "I'll never come home! Not as long as I am not Matt's child! You can tell him that! You can shout it out in Matt's Fort!"

"Thank you so much," said Little-Snip. "Not even Noddle-Pete would dare to come out with a message like that."

Talking of Noddle-Pete—he was poorly nowadays, Little-Snip told her. And why shouldn't he be, when everything else was so wretched? Matt scolded and grumbled morning, noon, and night. Nothing suited him any more, and the robbery business was going badly. The whole forest was teeming with soldiers. They had caught Pelle and put him in one of the sheriff's dungeons on bread and water. There were two of Borka's men there as well, and the sheriff had sworn, it was said, that all the robbers of Matt's Forest would be taken captive and receive their rightful punishment within a year and a day. And what would that mean? Little-Snip wondered. Death, perhaps?

"Doesn't he ever laugh nowadays?" asked Ronia.

Little-Snip looked surprised. "Who? The sheriff?"

"I'm talking about Matt," Ronia said.

And Little-Snip assured her that nobody had heard Matt laugh since the morning Ronia had leaped across Hell's Gap before his eyes.

Little-Snip had to go before it was too dark. He was going home now, and he was already worrying about what to say to Lovis.

So he tried again. "Ronia, come home! Please! Come home, won't you?"

Ronia shook her head and said, "Thank Lovis a thousand times for the bread!"

Little-Snip quickly thrust his fist in the leather bag. "Sakes alive, I've got a bag of salt for you too! I'd have been in deep trouble if I'd taken it home again."

Ronia took the bag of salt. "I have a mother who thinks of

everything! She knows what you need if you're to stay alive. But how did she know that we had only a few grains of salt left?"

"Perhaps that's the sort of thing a mother feels," said Little-Snip, "when her child lacks something she needs."

"Only a mother like Lovis," Ronia said.

She stood gazing for a long time at Little-Snip as he went away. She watched him speed nimbly along the narrow shelf of rock, and she did not return to the cave until he was out of sight.

"So you didn't go home with him to your father," said Birk. He was already lying on his bed of fir branches. Ronia could not see him in the darkness, but she heard the words, and they were enough to irritate her.

"I have no father," she said. "And if you don't watch out, I may have no brother either!"

"Forgive me, sister, if I'm unfair," said Birk. "But I sometimes know what you're thinking."

"Yes," said Ronia in the darkness, "I'm thinking that I've lived for eleven winters but the twelfth will be the death of me. And I'd so much like to stay on earth. If you can understand that!"

"Forget your winters," Birk said. "It's summer now!"

And it was summer. More and more summer every day, clearer, warmer than any summer they could remember. Every day in the noonday heat they bathed in the cold water of the river. They swam and dove like a pair of otters and allowed the current to carry them until the roar of Greedy Falls became so loud that it felt too near and too dangerous. Greedy Falls, where the river flung its mass of water out over a mighty precipice. No one got away alive after that journey.

Ronia and Birk knew where the danger began to be immediate.

"As soon as I catch a glimpse of Greedy Hump sticking out," said Ronia, "I know it's really dangerous."

Greedy Hump was a great boulder in the middle of the river some distance above the falls. It was a warning mark for Ronia and Birk. They knew then it was time to make for the bank, and that was hard and tiring. When they reached it, they lay panting and blue with cold, and let the sun warm them through while they watched the otters swimming and diving along the river's edge without ever tiring.

As the day cooled toward evening, they went out into the woods to ride. Villain and Savage had kept away for a time. The harpy had scared them so much that they were also frightened of the humans who had been sitting on their backs when they were hunted. They stayed shy for quite a long time, but now they seemed to have forgotten everything; now they came running and wanted to race again. Ronia and Birk let them gallop off their first energy and then rode far and wide through the forest.

"These warm summer evenings are lovely for riding," said Ronia. And she thought, Why can't it always be summer in the forest? And why can't I always be happy?

She loved her forest and all that was in it. All the trees, all the small lakes and springs and brooks they rode past, all the mossy outcroppings, all the wild strawberry patches and the blueberry bushes, all the flowers, animals, and birds—then why did it sometimes feel so melancholy, and why must it one day be winter?

"What are you thinking, sister mine?" asked Birk.

"I'm thinking that . . . there are murktrolls living under that enormous rock," said Ronia. "I saw them dancing there in springtime. And I like murktrolls and rumphobs, but not gray dwarfs and wild harpies, I'll have you know!"

"No, who does?" said Birk.

"But I hate harpies most," she said. "And it really is extraordinary that we have been left in peace here for so long. They can't know that we're living in the Bear's Cave."

"It's because they have their own caves in the mountains on the other side of the forest and not by the river," said Birk. "And perhaps the gray dwarfs have kept quiet for once—otherwise we'd have had the harpies down on us long ago."

Ronia shuddered. "It's not good to talk about them. We might bring them here."

It was getting dark more quickly now. The time of the light nights was over. In the evening they sat by their fire and saw pale stars sparkling in the sky. And as the darkness deepened, the stars became more and more brilliant, burning clear and bright over the woods. It was still a summer sky, but Ronia knew what the stars were saying: soon it will be autumn!

The next morning, another hot day, they bathed as usual. And then the harpies came. Not one or two but many of them, a great, fierce flock. Suddenly the air was filled with them, hovering above the river, screeching and hooting.

"Ho, ho! Lovely little humans in the water! Now the blood will run, ho, ho!"

"Dive, Ronia!" shouted Birk, and they dove and swam underwater until they had to come up for air. And when they saw the sky made dark by more and more harpies, they knew that it was hopeless now. This time they would not escape.

The harpies will see to it that I don't have to worry about the winter any more, Ronia thought bitterly, listening to the screeching, which never stopped.

"Lovely little humans in the water, now there will be clawing, now the blood will run, ho, ho!"

But wild harpies liked to frighten and torment before they went into the attack. Time enough for clawing and killing, but it was almost as much fun to fly around hooting and terrorizing, while they waited for the great harpy's sign that meant: it's time now! And the great harpy, the wildest and fiercest of them all, flew in wide sweeps over the river—ho, ho, she was in no hurry! But just wait, soon she would be the first of all to strike her claws in one of the creatures splashing in the water there. Should she take the one with black hair? The one with red hair was out of sight just now, but he was certain to pop up again soon. Ho, ho, there were many sharp claws waiting for him then, ho, ho!

Ronia dove and came up again, gasping for air. Her eyes searched about—where was Birk? She could not see him, she could not see him anywhere, and she moaned in despair. Where was he? Had he drowned? Had he left her alone with the harpies?

"Birk!" she screamed in terror. "Birk, where are you?"

Then the great harpy swooped, howling, down upon her, and Ronia closed her eyes. . . . Birk, my brother, how could you leave me alone at the worst time?

"Ho, ho," howled the harpy, "now the blood will run!"

But still she wanted to wait just a little longer, just a little, and then . . . ho, ho! She circled above the river once again and suddenly Ronia heard Birk's voice.

"Ronia, come quickly!"

A fallen birch, with green leaves still on its upper branches, came floating down on the current, and Birk was clinging to it. She could barely see his head above the water, but there he was. He had not left her alone! Oh, what a comfort that was!

But if she did not hurry now, the current would soon carry him out of reach. She dove and swam for her life . . . and then she had reached him. He stretched out his hand and pulled her to him, and there they hung, from the same branch, hidden as well as possible under the sheltering leaves of the birch tree.

"Oh, Birk," Ronia gasped, "I thought you'd drowned!"

"Not yet," said Birk, "but soon! Can you hear Greedy Falls?"

And Ronia heard the roar of mighty waters, the voice of Greedy Falls. They were now being carried to that abyss by the current. They were already far too close; Ronia knew it, she could see it. And their speed was increasing, and the thunder with it. Already she could feel the relentless tug of the falls. Soon, soon they would be flung out on the last journey, the one they could make only once.

And for that she wanted to be near Birk. She crept close against him and knew that he felt as she did: better the Greedy Falls than the harpies.

Birk put his arm over her shoulders. Whatever happened, they would be together, sister and brother. Nothing could part them now.

But the harpies were searching furiously. Where were the little humans? It was time now to start clawing. Why were there no little humans there any more?

There was only a tree with a leafy crown being carried rapidly down the river by the current. What was hidden under the green branches the harpies could not see, and, howling with rage, they circled and searched, circled and searched.

But Ronia and Birk were already far away, no longer able to hear their howls. They could hear only the thunder, which grew and grew, and they knew that they were very close to it now.

"Sister mine," said Birk.

Ronia could not hear him, but she could see from his lips what he was saying. And although neither of them could hear a word, they spoke to each other. They said what must be said before it was too late. How good it was to love someone so much that there was no need to fear even the most difficult thing. They spoke of it although neither of them could hear a single word.

But then they stopped talking altogether, simply held each other and closed their eyes.

Suddenly there came a violent jerk, which brought them to their senses. The birch had run straight into Greedy Hump. The impact made the birch branch swing around. It changed direction, and before the current could catch it again, it had traveled some way in toward the riverbank.

"Ronia, we're going to try," shouted Birk.

He pulled her free of the branch to which she was clinging. And in a moment they were both down in the foaming eddies. Now both of them had to fight for themselves, fight for their lives against the merciless current that was straining with all its strength to carry them to Greedy Falls. They could see the smooth water by the bank, so close. Near, but still much too far away.

Greedy Falls will win in the end, thought Ronia. She could do no more. She wanted to give up now, just sink and let herself be carried where the current took her and vanish over Greedy Falls.

But Birk was in front of her. He turned his head and looked at her. Time and again he turned to look at her and she tried again. Tried and tried until she could do no more.

But by then she had reached the smooth water, and Birk dragged her behind him to the bank. Then there was no more he could do, either.

"But we must . . . you must," he gasped.

And in the extreme of desperation they hauled themselves up on the bank. There in the heat of the sun they fell asleep at once, not even aware that they were saved.

It was not until the sun was sinking that they came home to the Bear's Cave. And there, on the platform outside, Lovis sat waiting for them.

Fifteen

"My child!" said Lovis. "How wet your hair is. Have you been swimming?"

Ronia stood still, looking at her mother. There she sat, leaning against the rock wall, steady and safe as the cliff itself. Ronia looked at her with love and wished that Lovis had come another time. Any time at all, but not now! Now she would have liked to be alone with Birk. It felt as if her soul were still fluttering inside her after all the ferocity and danger. Oh, if only she had had the chance to talk herself into calm with Birk and to be glad that they were alive, alone with him!

But there sat Lovis, her dear Lovis, whom she had not seen for such a long time. Her mother must not be allowed to feel unwelcome.

Ronia smiled at her. "Yes, we've been having a little swim, Birk and I."

Birk! Now she saw that he was already on his way into the cave, and she did not want that. It must not happen. She rushed after him and whispered, "Aren't you going to come and say hello to my mother?"

Birk looked at her coldly. "You don't say hello to uninvited guests. My mother taught me that when she was still carrying me in her arms!"

Ronia gasped. It hurt to be so furious and so desperate. There he stood, Birk, looking at her with ice-cold eyes, the same Birk she had been so close to just now and whom she had wanted to follow even down Greedy Falls. Now he turned away from her and became a stranger. Oh, how she detested him for that! She had never known such rage before! For that matter, it was not only Birk she loathed, when she came to think of it. She loathed everything, just everything, everything and everyone that pulled and tugged at her until she was nearly torn in half, Birk and Lovis and Matt and the harpies and the Bear's Cave and the forest and the summer and the winter and that Undis who had taught Birk stupid things when he was an infant and those horrible harpies . . . No, wait, she had already dealt with those! But there were other things she loathed until she could have screamed, even if she happened to have forgotten for the moment what they were, but scream she would, and scream she should, until the mountains rang!

No, she did not scream. She just hissed at Birk before he disappeared into the cave, "It's a pity your mother didn't teach you some manners, too, while she was about it."

She went back to Lovis and began to explain. Birk was tired, she said, and then she was silent. She sank down on the rocky platform beside her mother, and with her face buried against Lovis's knee she cried, not until the mountains rang, but just a quiet little cry that could not be heard.

"You know why I have come," said Lovis.

And Ronia muttered through her tears, "Not to give me bread, I suppose?"

"No," said Lovis, stroking her hair. "You'll get bread when you come home."

Ronia sobbed again. "I'll never come home."

"Well, then it will end with Matt jumping in the river," Lovis said calmly.

Ronia lifted her head. "Would he jump in the river for my sake? But he won't even mention my name!"

"Not when he's awake," said Lovis, "but every night he cries in his sleep and calls for you."

"How do you know?" asked Ronia. "Have you got him back in your bed now? Isn't he sleeping with Noddle-Pete any more?"

"No," said Lovis. "Noddle-Pete couldn't stand having him there any longer, and I can scarcely stand it either. But he has to have someone to hang on to when things get really bad."

She was silent for a long time; then she said, "You know, Ronia, it's hard to see someone being so inhumanly tortured."

Ronia felt it was about to burst out now, that crying that was going to make the mountains ring, but she clenched her teeth and then said quietly, "Look, Lovis, if you were a child and had a father who denied you so completely that he would not even say your name, would you go back to him? Supposing he didn't even come and ask you?"

Lovis thought for a moment. "No, I wouldn't. He would have to ask—that he would!"

"And Matt never will," said Ronia.

Once again she hid her face against Lovis's knee and made her rough yellow gown wet with silent tears.

Night and darkness had fallen; even the worst days come to an end.

"You go to bed, Ronia," said Lovis. "I'll wait here and drop off from time to time, and as soon as it's light I'll go home again."

"I want to sleep by you," said Ronia. "And you must sing the Wolf Song!"

She remembered how she herself had tried to sing the Wolf Song for Birk. But she had soon tired of it, and she had no intention of singing any other songs for him as long as she lived.

But Lovis sang, and the world became as it should be. Ronia sank into the deep peace of childhood, and with her head against Lovis's knee she fell asleep under the stars and did not wake until the morning was bright.

Lovis had already gone, but she had not taken her gray shawl with her; she had wrapped it around Ronia. Ronia could feel the warmth of it as soon as she woke up, and she breathed in the scent. Yes, that's Lovis, she thought; her shawl smells a little like that little rabbit I had once.

Over by the fire Birk was sitting hunched with his head on his arms, his copper hair hanging forward, hiding his face. There he sat, looking so hopelessly forlorn that it hurt Ronia. She forgot everything else, and with the shawl trailing after her, she went over to him. But she hesitated a little; perhaps he would like to be left in peace.

In the end she had to ask, "What is it, Birk?"

He looked up at her and smiled. "I'm sitting here grieving, sister mine!"

"Why?" asked Ronia.

"I'm grieving because you are fully and completely my sister only when Greedy Falls is calling you, but not otherwise. Not when your father calls through his various messengers. And so I behave like a coward, and I'm grieving about that too, if you must know."

Who is not grieving? thought Ronia. Shouldn't I grieve when what I do pleases no one?

"But it's not fair of me to blame you for that." Birk went on. "It's as it has to be—I know that."

Ronia looked at him shyly. "Do you want to be my brother in any case?"

"Yes, that's just it," said Birk. "I am your brother fully and completely and always, and you know it! But now you must also know why I wanted us to have this summer in peace without any messengers from Matt's Fort, and why I cannot bear to talk about the winter."

Truly, there was nothing Ronia wanted to know more. She had wondered a lot why Birk was not worrying at all about the winter. "It is summer now, sister mine," he would say, as calmly as if winter would never come.

"We have only this summer, you and I," said Birk, "and the way things are with me now, I don't mind very much about living unless you are with me. And when winter comes you won't be with me. You must go back to Matt's Fort then."

"And what about you?" asked Ronia. "Where will you be?"

"Here," Birk said. "Of course I could go and beg my way back into Borka's Keep—I wouldn't be driven away, I know. But what good would that do? I'd still be without you. I wouldn't even be allowed to see you. So I'm going to stay in the Bear's Cave."

"And freeze to death," said Ronia.

Birk laughed. "Perhaps, perhaps not! I have worked out that you might come skiing down now and then with a little bread and salt and with my wolfskin, if you can get it out of Borka's Keep."

Ronia shook her head. "If it's like last winter, I couldn't manage to ski. I couldn't even get down to the Wolf's Neck. And if it's like last winter and you are living in the Bear's Cave, it will be the end of you, Birk Borkason!"

"Then that's how it will have to be," said Birk. "But it's summer now, sister mine!"

Ronia looked at him gravely. "Summer or winter—who said I was going back to Matt's Fort?"

"I did," said Birk. "Even if I have to carry you there myself. I plan to freeze to death on my own, if it has to be. But as I said, it's summer now!"

Summer would not last forever; he knew it and Ronia knew it. But now they began to live as if it would, and as far as possible they pushed away all painful thoughts of winter. They wanted to make the most of every hour from dawn to dusk and nighttime and draw the sweetness from it. The days could come and go; they were living in a summer enchantment and would not be disturbed. They had just a little time left.

"And no one is going to spoil that," said Birk.

Ronia agreed with him. "I'm drinking in the summer like the wild bee sucking up honey," she said. "I'm gathering it together in a big lump of summer, to live on when . . . when it's not summer any more. Do you know what there is in it?"

And she told Birk, "It's a whole batch of sunrises, and blueberry bushes covered with berries, and the freckles you have on your arms, and moonlight over the river in the evening, and starry skies, and the woods in the noonday heat when the sun is shining on the fir trees, and the small rain in the evening, and squirrels and foxes and hares and elk and all the wild horses we know, and when we swim and when we ride in the woods—well, it's a whole batch of everything that is summer!"

"You're a good summer baker," said Birk. "Keep it up!"

They spent all the hours from morning to evening in their woods. They fished and hunted to get what they needed to eat, but otherwise they lived in peace with all the life about them. They took long walks to watch animals and birds, climbed rocks and trees, rode and swam in lakes in the forest where no harpies disturbed them—and the days of summer passed.

The sky was growing clearer and cooler. One or two cold nights came, and suddenly there were yellow leaves in the crown of a birch tree down by the river. They saw them as they sat by their fire early one morning, but they said nothing about it.

And new days came with more and more sharpness and clarity in the air. You could see for miles across the green woods, but now there was much yellow and red among the green, and soon the whole riverside was flaming gold and red. They sat by their fire and saw the beauty of it, but they said nothing about it.

There was more mist over the river than before, and one evening when they had to go down to the stream for water, the mist had risen over the forest. Suddenly they were in the midst of the densest fog. Birk set down his bucket of water and seized Ronia firmly by the arm.

"What's this?" said Ronia. "Are you afraid of the fog? Don't you think we'll find our way home?"

Birk did not tell her what he was afraid of, but he waited. And suddenly from far away in the forest came that plaintive song he remembered so well.

Ronia stood still and listened. "Do you hear? It is the Unearthly Ones singing! At last I can hear them!"

"Have you never heard them before?" asked Birk.

"No, never," said Ronia. "They want to lure us down to the Underworld—did you know that?"

"I know," said Birk. "Would you like to follow them there?"

Ronia laughed. "I'm not mad, you know! But Noddle-Pete said . . ." She stopped.

"What did Noddle-Pete say?" Birk asked.

"Oh, it doesn't matter," said Ronia.

But as they stood there and waited for the mist to lift a little so they could make their way home, she thought of what Noddle-Pete had once said.

"When the Unearthly Ones come up into the forest and sing, you know it is autumn. And then it will soon be winter—oh, dear me, yes!"

Sixteen

NODDLE-PETE WAS RIGHT. WHEN THE UNEARTHLY ONES CAME UP into the forest with their laments, it was autumn. Even if Birk and Ronia did not want to admit it. Summer had died slowly. The autumn rains set in with such stubbornness that even Ronia was upset, although she usually liked rain.

They sat in the cave for days on end, listening to the endless splashing on the platform outside. In weather like this they could not even keep the fire going, and it was so cold that they had to go out into the forest at last and try to run themselves warm. They got a little warmer, but very wet. Once home in the cave again, they wrung out their soaking clothes and, wrapped in their fur skins, they sat watching for even the slightest sign of lightness in the sky.

But all they could see through the cave opening was a wall of rain.

"It's a rainy summer we're having," said Birk. "But of course it will get better!"

And it did stop raining at last, but then storms came thundering over the forest. Winds tore up fir trees and ripped the leaves off the birches. The golden gleam was gone; on the slope down by the river there was nothing to be seen now but bare trees swaying pitifully in the harsh blast that was trying to tear them from their roots.

"It's a blowy summer we're having," said Birk, "but of course it will get better!"

It did not get better. It got worse. The cold came, and it grew colder every day. And now the thoughts of winter could not be kept at bay any longer, not by Ronia at least. She often had nightmares. One night she dreamed she saw Birk lying embedded in snow, his face white and his hair white, too, with frost. She woke up with a scream. It was already morning, and Birk was busy outside with the fire. She rushed to him and was relieved when she saw that he still had his usual red hair, with no frost on it.

But the woods on the other side of the river were now white with frost for the first time.

"It's a frosty summer we're having," said Birk with a grin.

Ronia gave him a resentful look. How could he be so calm? How could he speak so lightly? Didn't he realize? Didn't he mind at all about his poor life? It was wrong to be afraid in Matt's Forest—she knew that—but now she was beginning to be afraid, terribly afraid of what would happen to them when winter came.

"My sister is not happy," said Birk. "It's nearly time for her to leave here and warm herself at some other fire than mine."

Then she went back into the cave and lay down on her bed again. Another fire—but she had no other fire to go to! He meant the fire at home in the stone hall, and sure enough, she longed for it in this villainous cold—oh, how she longed for once in her life to be warm again! But she could not go to Matt's Fort, since she was not Matt's child. The fire at home would never warm her again, she knew, and that was that! There was nothing to be done. What was the use of grumbling when there was no escape?

She saw that the bucket was empty. She would have to go down to the spring for water.

"I'll come as soon as I get the fire going," Birk called after her. Carrying the water home was hard work. It required two of them.

Ronia walked off along the narrow path on the mountainside, where you had to go carefully and watch out that you did not fall headfirst off the rocks. Then she ran the last little bit through the forest between birches and fir trees to the glade where the spring was. But before she had quite reached it she stopped dead. Someone was sitting on the stone beside the spring! Matt was sitting there, Matt and none other! She remembered that dark, curly head so vividly that her heart shook in her body. And now she began to cry, standing there among the birch trees, crying silently to herself. Then she saw that Matt, too, was crying. Just like the time in her dream, he was sitting alone in the woods, grieving and crying. He had not noticed her yet, but suddenly he raised his eyes and caught sight of her. At once he flung one arm across his eyes and hid his tears, a gesture so helpless and despairing that she could not bear to see it. With a cry she rushed forward and threw herself into his arms.

"My child!" whispered Matt. "My child!"

Then he shouted, "I have my child!"

Ronia wept into his beard and asked, sobbing, "Am I your child now, Matt? Am I really your child again?"

And Matt cried and answered, "Yes, as you have always been, my Ronia! My child, whom I have wept for night and day. My God, how I've suffered!"

He held her a little away from him so that he could see her face. Then he asked tenderly, "Is it as Lovis said, that you will come home only if I ask you to?"

Ronia was silent. And at that moment she saw Birk. There he stood among the birch trees, white-faced, his eyes full of sadness. He must not be so unhappy—*Birk, my brother, what are you thinking when you look like that?*

"Is it true, Ronia? Will you come home with me now?" Matt asked.

Ronia was silent, looking at Birk--*Birk, my brother, do you remember Greedy Falls?*

"Come, Ronia, we're going now," said Matt.

And Birk knew as he stood there that now it was time. Time to say good-bye and let Ronia go back to Matt, with thanks for the loan. It had to be; he himself had wished it. And he had known it for a long time, so why did it hurt so much? *Ronia, you don't know how it feels, but do it quickly! Go now!*

"Though I haven't asked you yet," said Matt. "I do it now. I ask you, Ronia, with all my heart, come home to me again!"

Nothing in my life has ever been so hard, Ronia thought. She must say it now—it would crush Matt, she knew, but she must say it. That she wanted to stay with Birk. That she *could not* leave him alone to freeze to death in the winter forest—*Birk, my brother, nothing can part us in life or death, don't you know that?*

Only then did Matt catch sight of Birk, and he sighed heavily. But then he shouted, "Birk Borkason, come here! I want a word with you!"

Birk approached reluctantly and no closer than necessary. He gave Matt a defiant look and asked, "What do you want?"

"To give you a beating, really," Matt said. "But I'm not going to. Instead, I ask you with all my heart, come back to Matt's Fort with us now! It's not because I like you—don't think that, whatever you do! But my daughter does—I know that now—and perhaps I can learn too. I have had time to think about this and that these last months!"

When Ronia fully realized what he had said, she began to quiver all over. She felt something break free within her. That awful lump of ice she had been carrying inside her—how was it that with just a few words her father could make it melt like a brook in spring? How could the miracle have suddenly happened and she no longer had to choose between Birk and Matt? The two she loved—now she need not lose either of them! The miracle had happened, just here and just now!

Full of gladness and love and thankfulness, she looked at Matt and then at Birk. Then she saw that Birk was not happy at all. He looked confused and suspicious, and she grew frightened. He could be so stubborn and pigheaded. What if he did not know what was good for him? What if he would not come with them?

"Matt," she said, "I must talk to Birk alone."

"Why?" asked Matt. "Oh, well, I'll go and have a look at my old

Bear's Cave meanwhile. But be quick, because we must go home now."

"We must go home now," Birk said scornfully when Matt had gone. "What home? Does he think I am going to be the whipping boy for Matt's robbers? Never!"

"Whipping boy! How stupid you are," said Ronia, and now she was furious again. "Would you rather freeze to death in the Bear's Cave?"

Birk was silent for a moment; then he said, "Yes, I think so!"

Then Ronia became desperate. "Life is something you have to take care of—don't you realize that? And if you stay in the Bear's Cave for the winter, you'll be throwing away your life! And mine!"

"Why do you say that?" asked Birk. "How can I throw away your life?"

Ronia shouted furiously, "Because I would stay with *you*, you numskull! Whether you liked it or not!"

Birk stood silently looking at her for a long time. Then he said, "Do you know what you're saying now, Ronia?"

"I know," Ronia shouted, "that nothing can part us! And you know it too, numskull!"

Then Birk smiled his brightest smile, and he was handsome when he smiled.

"I don't want to throw away your life, sister mine! It's the last thing I want. I will go with you wherever you go. Even if I have to live among Matt's robbers until it chokes me!"

They had put out the fire and packed everything. Now they wer. leaving the Bear's Cave, and that was hard. But Ronia whispered to Birk, so that Matt would not hear her and begin to worry unnecessarily, "Next spring we'll move back again!"

"Yes, because we'll still be alive," said Birk, looking as if the idea pleased him.

Matt was pleased too. He walked ahead of them through the forest, singing so that all the wild horses in their way fled off, startled, through the trees. All but Villain and Savage. They stood still, waiting, probably imagining that they were going to run some more races.

"Not today," said Ronia, stroking Villain. "But tomorrow, perhaps. Perhaps every day if there isn't too much snow!"

And Birk patted Savage. "Yes, we'll be coming back! Just you stay alive!"

They could see that the horses already had thicker coats: soon they would be all shaggy for protection against the cold. Villain and Savage would also live to see another spring.

But Matt was far ahead of them, walking through the forest singing, and they had to hurry to catch up with him. And when they had walked for a long time, they came to the Wolf's Neck. There Birk stopped.

"Matt," he said, "I want to go home to Borka's Keep first and see how things are with Undis and Borka. But I give you my thanks for allowing me to come to Matt's Fort and meet Ronia whenever I like."

"Yes, yes," said Matt. "It won't be easy for me, but come!"

Then he laughed. "You know what Noddle-Pete says? The old fool thinks that the sheriff and his men will win in the end if we don't watch out. And therefore, he says, the best thing would be for Matt's robbers and Borka's robbers to join forces—yes, he has plenty of crazy ideas, the old idiot!"

He gave Birk a look of sympathy "It's a shame that you should have such a dirty devil of a father—otherwise one might at least be able to think it over."

"Dirty devil yourself," said Birk kindly, and Matt laughed appreciatively.

Birk gave Ronia his hand. It was here, below the Wolf's Neck, that they had always said good-bye.

"I'll be seeing you, robber's daughter! Every day, you know that, sister mine!"

Ronia nodded. "Every day, Birk Borkason!"

You could have heard a pin drop among the robbers in the stone hall when Matt and Ronia walked in. No one dared to cheer; it was a long time since their chieftain had allowed any cheers in Matt's Fort. Only Noddle-Pete made what was for his age an unnaturally high leap of joy.

"There should be *some* sort of greeting when folk come home," he said. And at that Matt laughed so heartily and so long that the robbers' eyes filled with tears of happiness. It was the first laughter they had heard from Matt since that miserable morning at Hell's Gap, and the robbers hastened to join in. They laughed until they doubled up; Ronia as well. But then Lovis came in from the sheep pen, and there was silence. You could not laugh at the sight of a mother greeting her lost child who has just come home, and the robbers' eyes filled with tears at this too.

"Lovis, can you bring in the big washtub for me?" asked Ronia.

Lovis nodded. "Yes, I'm already heating the water!"

"I believe you," said Ronia. "You're the kind of mother that thinks of everything. And you have never seen a filthier child!"

"No, never," said Lovis.

Ronia lay in her bed, full and clean and warm. She had eaten Lovis's bread and drunk some milk, and then Lovis had scrubbed her in the washtub until her skin glowed. Now she lay there in the same old bed, and between the curtains she saw the fire slowly burning down on the hearth. Everything was as it used to be. Lovis had sung the Wolf Song for her and Matt. It was time to sleep. And Ronia was sleepy, but her thoughts were wandering.

It will be very cold in the Bear's Cave now, she thought. And here I lie, warm right down to my toes. Isn't it strange that such a little thing can make you feel happy! Then she thought about Birk and wondered how he was getting on over at Borka's Keep. I hope he's warm right down to his toes too, she thought, and closed her eyes. I'll ask him tomorrow.

There was silence in the stone hall. But then came an anxious cry from Matt.

"Ronia!"

"What is it?" she murmured, half asleep.

"I just wanted to hear that you were really there," said Matt.

"Of course I'm here," mumbled Ronia.

And then she slept.

Seventeen

THE WOODS THAT RONIA LOVED, THE AUTUMN WOODS AND THE WINTER woods, they were her friends again now. In the last weeks in the Bear's Cave she had felt them to be threatening and hostile, but now she went riding with Birk in a frosty forest that gave her nothing but joy, and she told Birk all about it.

"As long as you know that you are going to be warm right down to your toes when you come home, you can be in the woods in all weathers. But not if you have to lie shivering in a cold cave afterward."

And Birk, who had planned to spend the winter in the Bear's Cave, was now very glad to warm himself by the fire at home in Borka's Keep.

That was where he must live, he knew, and Ronia knew it too. Otherwise there would be still more enmity in the fort on Matt's Mountain.

"And you know, they were so extraordinarily glad, Undis and Borka, when I came home," said Birk. "I would never have believed they cared so much about me."

"Yes, you must live with them," said Ronia. "Until spring!"

It was welcome news to Matt, too, that Birk was to stay at home.

"Of course, of course," he told Lovis, "that little thief hound can come and go here as he likes. I invited him to come home with us, after all. But it's a relief not to have to see that red head of his all the time!"

Life in Matt's Fort went on, and now it was jolly there again. The robbers sang and danced, and Matt laughed his bellowing laugh as before.

And yet the robber life was not exactly as it had been. The fight against the sheriff's men had grown tougher, and Matt knew that they were really after him now. And he explained why to Ronia.

"Just because we took Pelle out of that miserable dungeon one dark night—and two of Borka's thieving dogs at the same time."

"Little-Snip thought Pelle was going to be hanged," said Ronia.

"No one hangs my robbers," said Matt. "And now I've taught that rascally Pelle that robbers don't stay where you put them!"

But Noddle-Pete shook his bald head thoughtfully. "And that's why we've got the soldiers swarming through the woods like cattle flies. And the sheriff will win in the end, Matt—how many times must I tell you?"

There he went again, old Noddle-Pete, nagging about Matt and

Borka being reconciled before it was too late. A single, strong band of robbers might be able to handle the sheriff and all his merry men, but never two separate bands who wasted most of their time cheating each other and fighting over the plunder like wolves over morsels of flesh, said Noddle-Pete.

This was not the kind of thing Matt liked to hear. It was quite enough for him to worry about it from time to time.

"You speak what you think, old man," said Matt. "Of course, you're right in a way. But who do you think would be chief of that robber band?" He gave a jeering laugh. "Borka, eh? I, Matt, am the strongest and mightiest robber chieftain in all the mountains and forests, and I intend to remain so! But we can't be sure that Borka will understand that."

"Show him, then," said Noddle-Pete. "You ought to be able to win in single combat with him, you great ox!"

This was what Noddle-Pete had thought out in lonely hours of scheming. A single combat that would put Borka in his place and make him reasonable; then they would have a single robber band in Matt's Fort, with everyone helping to lure the soldiers onto the wrong track and lead them a dog's life until they got tired of hunting robbers. Wasn't that a cunning idea?

"I think the most cunning idea of all would be to stop robbing," said Ronia. "I've always thought so."

Noddle-Pete smiled his friendly, toothless smile at her.

"You're quite right about that, Ronia. You're very bright. But I am too old and feeble to drum something like that into Matt's skull."

Matt looked at him in annoyance. "And *you* can say that—you who were once a bold robber yourself, first under my father and then under me! Stop robbing! What would we live on then—have you thought about that?"

"Have you never noticed," asked Noddle-Pete, "that there are people who are not robbers and yet they manage to live?"

"Yes, but *how*?" Matt said sourly.

Well, there were several ways, Noddle-Pete explained. "I know something I could teach you if I didn't know that you are and will remain a robber until you're hanged. But all in good time I'll tell Ronia a nice little secret."

"What sort of secret?" Matt asked.

"As I just said," said Noddle-Pete, "I'll tell Ronia so she won't be left helpless on the day you're hanged."

"Hanged, hanged, be hanged!" Matt said angrily. "Now be quiet, you miserable old croak!"

The days passed, and Matt did not listen to Noddle-Pete's advice. But early one morning, before Matt's robbers had gotten around to saddling their horses, Borka came riding up to the Wolf's Neck and asked to speak to Matt. He came with bad news. And since his archenemy had so generously rescued two of Borka's men from the sheriff's dungeon not long ago, he wanted to render a service in return and warn Matt. Today no robber who valued his life should poke his nose into the woods, said Borka. Things had reached a pretty pass again. He had just come from Robbers' Walk, where the soldiers had been lying in ambush. They had managed to capture two of his men, and a third had been badly wounded by an arrow when he tried to escape.

"Those brutes begrudge a poor robber his living," Borka said bitterly.

Matt frowned. "We'll have to teach them to mind their manners! We can't have this sort of thing!"

It was only afterward that he realized he had said "we," and he sighed heavily. For a while he stood in silence, looking Borka up and down.

"Perhaps we should . . . join forces," he said at last, although his own words made him shudder. Fancy talking like that to a Borka! How his father and grandfather and great-grandfather would toss and turn in their graves if they heard him!

But Borka looked more cheerful. "For once in your life you said something quite clever then, Matt! *One* strong band of robbers—that would be good! Under *one* strong chief! I know one who would do," he said, drawing himself up. "Strong and resourceful as I am!"

Then Matt let out a terrible laugh. "Come on, you, and I'll show you who would do as chief!"

So Noddle-Pete got what he wanted. There would be a single combat; Matt and Borka had finally decided it was a good idea. The excitement grew among their men as this remarkable news reached them, and on the morning of the fight Matt's robbers were making such a noise in the stone hall that Lovis had to drive them out.

"Out!" she shouted. "I simply can't listen to this row!"

It was enough to listen to Matt. He was striding up and down the stone hall, grinding his teeth and bragging about how he was going to batter Borka to bits until even Undis would not recognize him.

Noddle-Pete sniggered. "Brag when you're riding home—that's what my mother always said."

And Ronia stared with displeasure at her hotheaded father. "I don't want to watch when you're doing the battering!"

"You won't be allowed to," Matt said. Women and children were kept away; that was the custom. It was not thought to be good for them to see what happened at a "wild beasts' match," as trials of strength like this were called, and the violence that went on at them was reason enough for the name.

"But you're going to be there in any event, Noddle-Pete," said Matt. "I know you've been feeling poorly, but a wild beasts' match will put heart into you. Come on, old man, I'll put you on my horse. The time has come!"

It was a cold, sunny morning with frost on the ground, and in the open space below the Wolf's Neck stood Matt's robbers and Borka's robbers with their spears, forming a ring around Matt and Borka. Now they were going to find out who would make the better chief.

On top of a rocky outcrop close by sat Noddle-Pete, wrapped in a fur. He looked like a bedraggled old crow, but his eyes were shining with expectation, and he was eagerly following what was happening below.

The two champions had removed everything except their shirts and were now stamping around barefoot on the frosty ground. They felt and tensed their arm muscles and kicked out with their legs in all directions to limber up.

"You're looking a bit blue around the nose, Borka," said Matt. "But you'll be warm soon, I promise you!"

"And I promise you the same," Borka assured him.

In wild beasts' matches every kind of trick and dirty hold was allowed. You could break and bore, rip and tear, bite and scratch; you could kick with your bare feet, too, but not between the legs. That was regarded as an outrage, and anyone who did it lost the fight forthwith.

But now Fooloks gave the sign they were waiting for. It was time to begin, and, uttering war cries, Matt and Borka rushed forward at each other.

"It's a great sorrow to me," said Matt, flinging his bear's arms around Borka's body, "that you're such a dirty devil"—here he squeezed, but only enough to make Borka begin to sweat a bit—"otherwise I might have made you my second-in-command long ago"—he took a more ferocious grip—"and not had to squeeze the kidneys out of you now"—here he crushed Borka's ribs till he rattled.

But when Borka had finished rattling, he drove his hard skull forcibly against Matt's nose so that the blood spurted.

"It's a great sorrow to *me*," said Borka, "that I've got to smash your snout"—he drove in another attack—"because you were as ugly as anyone could wish already"—now he grabbed one of Matt's ears and pulled. "Two ears—do you need more than one?" he asked, and pulled again.

But as the ear was just beginning to come loose, he lost his grip, for Matt simultaneously sent him sprawling and with an iron-hard fist pressed his face down until it felt much flatter than before. "I'm extraordinarily sorry," said Matt, "to have to batter you until Undis will cry every time she sees you by daylight!" He pressed again, but now Borka succeeded in getting a little piece of Matt's palm between his teeth, and he bit.

Matt gave a yell and tried to snatch his hand away, but Borka hung on until he had to stop for lack of breath. Then he spat a few small scraps of skin in Matt's face. "Here you are—take them home to the cat," he said, but he was puffing and blowing, because now Matt was lying with his full weight on top of him. And it was soon obvious that even if Borka had strong teeth, as far as the rest of his strength was concerned, he was no match for Matt.

When the fight was over, Matt stood there, the chief now, bloody-faced and with what was left of his shirt fluttering in rags around his body. Nevertheless, he was every inch a chieftain. All the robbers had to admit it, even though it was a mournful moment for some, especially Borka.

Borka was much the worse for wear and close to tears, so Matt thought he would give him a few words of comfort.

"Brother Borka—yes, from now on we're brothers," he said. "You shall keep a chieftain's name and fame all the days of your life, and you can carry on with your own men. But don't forget that Matt is the mightiest chieftain in all the mountains and woods, and my word counts for more than yours from now on—you know that!"

Borka nodded dumbly. He was not feeling particularly talkative at that moment.

But on the same evening Matt held a feast in the stone hall for the robbers of Matt's Fort, both his own and Borka's, a splendid banquet, with plenty of food and a good deal of beer.

And as the evening went on, Matt and Borka became more and more like brothers. Now laughing, now crying, they sat side by side at the long table and remembered their childhood when they had hunted rats together in the old pigsty. Many other amusing things they had done together were now remembered and described. All the robbers listened with relish, roaring with laughter, and Birk and Ronia, sitting at the far end of the table, enjoyed hearing it too. Their laughter shrilled high and clear above the rough voices of the robbers, and it was a joy to Matt and Borka to hear them. For a long, hard time there had been no Ronia and no Birk to laugh in Matt's Fort, and Matt and Borka had still scarcely gotten accustomed to the joy of having them home again. So that laughter was like the sweetest music in their ears, and it encouraged them to relate even more of their childhood doings.

But suddenly Matt said, "Don't be upset, Borka, because things went badly for you today. Better times may come for the Borka clan. When you and I are no longer there, your son will be chief, I should think, because my daughter does not want to be, and when she says no, it is no. She gets that from her mother!"

Borka looked absolutely delighted to hear this, but Ronia called all the way up the table, "So you think Birk wants to be a robber chieftain?"

"He does," said Borka positively.

Then Birk strode across the floor and stopped where everyone could see him. He raised his right hand and swore a solemn oath that never would he become a robber, no matter what happened.

A dismal silence fell over the stone hall. Borka sat there, tearfully bemoaning the son who had let them down so unnaturally. But Matt tried to comfort him.

"I have had to get used to it," he said, "and you will have to, too. You can't do anything with children these days. They do as they like—you just have to get used to it. But it's not easy."

The two chieftains sat for a long time, gazing gloomily into a future in which their proud robbers' life would be no more than a legend.

Only gradually did they return to the memories of rat hunts in the pigsty and decide to enjoy themselves in spite of their headstrong children. And their robbers competed with one another in banishing all gloom with cheerful songs and vigorous dances. They whirled until the floorboards creaked. Birk and Ronia joined in their dancing, and Ronia taught Birk many a joyous robbers' leap.

Throughout all this, Lovis and Undis sat in a room apart, eating, drinking, and chatting. Their tastes and ideas were different in almost every way. There was only one thing they agreed on: how truly wonderful it was to be able to rest their ears from time to time and not have to hear so much as a single squeak from any menfolk.

But in the stone hall the feast went on, until Noddle-Pete suddenly fell to the floor with exhaustion. He had had a glad and merry day despite his age, but now he could do no more, and Ronia helped him to his bedroom. There, tired and content, he sank down on his bed, and Ronia tucked the fur rug around him.

"It soothes my old heart," said Noddle-Pete, "that neither you nor Birk want to be a robber. It was something you could do with pleasure once upon a time—I won't deny it. But it's tougher now, and you can be hanged before you know it."

"Yes, and people scream and sob when you take their things away from them," Ronia said. "I'd never be able to stand that."

"No, my child, you'd never be able to stand that," said Noddle-Pete. "But now I'm going to tell you a nice little secret, if you promise never to tell it to a living soul except one!"

Ronia promised.

Then Noddle-Pete took hold of her two warm little hands to warm his own, which were very cold. "My little pride and joy," he said, "when I was young and spent my time in the woods just like you, I happened one day to save the life of a little gray dwarf whom the harpies were determined to tear to pieces. Of course, gray dwarfs are riffraff, but this one was a bit different, and he was so grateful afterward that I could scarcely get rid of him. He insisted on giving me . . . Well, here comes Matt," said Noddle-Pete, for Matt was standing in the doorway now and wanted to know why Ronia had stayed away so long. The feast was over and it was time for the Wolf Song.

"First I must hear the rest of this story," said Ronia.

And as Matt stood obstinately waiting, Noddle-Pete whispered the rest in her ear.

"Good," said Ronia when she had heard it all.

Night came and soon the whole of Matt's Fort and all its rascally robbers were asleep. But Matt was complaining bitterly as he lay in bed. Of course Lovis had smoothed ointment onto all his wounds and bruises, but it was no use. Now he had time to be aware of them, and his injuries hurt him horribly if he so much as twitched his little toe. He was quite unable to sleep, and it annoyed him that Lovis lay there sleeping peacefully. At last he woke her up.

"I'm in terrible pain," he said, "and my one hope is that that villain Borka is lying there hurting worse than me!"

Lovis turned toward the wall.

"Men!" she said, and fell back asleep at once.

Eighteen

"OLD PEOPLE HAVE NO BUSINESS TO GO AND FREEZE THEMSELVES TO the bone at wild beasts' matches," Lovis said sternly, when next day it became obvious that Noddle-Pete had the aches and shivers all over and did not want to get up. Even after he had gotten over the shivers completely, he refused to leave his bed.

"I might just as well lie here and stare as sit up and stare," he said.

Matt came to his room every day to let him know how the new robber life was getting on. Matt himself was pleased. Borka was doing a good job, he said, and wasn't too loud-mouthed either. Actually, he had his wits about him, and together they were now bringing in one fine haul after another. They fooled the sheriff's men—oh, it was a joy to see!—and soon Matt's Forest would be free of all those trashy soldiers.

"Brag when you're riding home," muttered Noddle-Pete, but Matt did not listen to him. He didn't have much time to sit there, in any case.

"You scrawny old dodderer," he said tenderly, patting Noddle-Pete before he left. "Try to get a bit of meat on your bones so they're strong enough to stand on!"

And Lovis did what she could. She brought hot, strengthening soups and other things that Noddle-Pete liked.

"Get that soup inside you to make you warm," she said. But not even the hottest soup could drive the chill from Noddle-Pete's bones, and Lovis was worried.

"We'll have to take him into the stone hall and warm him up," she told Matt one evening. And borne in Matt's strong arms, Noddle-Pete left his solitary bedroom. He was to share the bed with Matt. Lovis moved over to Ronia and shared her bed.

"At last, poor old thing that I am, I'll just about begin to thaw out," Noddle-Pete said.

Matt was as warm as glowing embers, and Noddle-Pete crept close to him like a child seeking warmth and comfort from his mother.

"Don't squash me," said Matt, but Noddle-Pete continued to creep close in spite of him. And when morning came, he refused to move back to his room. He liked this bed and he would stay in it. He could lie there watching Lovis at work as the day went by; it was here that the robbers gathered around him and described their deeds when they came home at night, and Ronia came too and told him about the time she and Birk had spent out in their woods. Noddle-Pete was happy.

"This is the way I like it while I'm waiting," he said.

"What are you waiting for?" Matt asked.

"Well, what do you think?" said Noddle-Pete.

Matt was unable to guess, but he noticed that bit by bit Noddle-Pete seemed to be crumbling away. He asked Lovis anxiously, "What do you think is the matter with him?"

"Old age," said Lovis.

Matt gave her a worried look. "But he won't die of it, will he?"

"Yes, he will," said Lovis.

Matt burst into tears. "No, no, be quiet!" he shouted. "I'll never stand for that!"

Lovis shook her head. "You decide a lot of things, Matt, but you won't be deciding this!"

Ronia, too, was worried about Noddle-Pete, and as he faded away she spent more and more time with him. Now he usually lay with closed eyes, opening them only occasionally to look at her. Then he smiled and said, "My joy and gladness, you won't forget what you know, will you?"

"No! If only I find the right place," said Ronia.

"You will," Noddle-Pete assured her. "When the time comes, you'll find it."

"Yes, of course I will," she said.

Time passed, and Noddle-Pete grew weaker and weaker. At last there came a night when they were all watching over him, Matt and Lovis and Ronia and the robbers. Noddle-Pete lay there unmoving, his eyes closed. Matt searched anxiously for any sign of life. But the bed was in shadow despite the light from the fire and the candle Lovis had lit. It was impossible to see any sign of life, and suddenly Matt bellowed, "He's dead!"

Then Noddle-Pete opened one eye and gave him a reproachful look. "I most certainly am not! Don't you think I have enough manners to say good-bye before I go away?"

Then he closed his eyes again for a long time, and they stood in silence, hearing only a few small, wheezing breaths.

"But now," said Noddle-Pete, opening his eyes, "now, my friends, I take leave of you all! Now I shall die."

And so he died.

Ronia had never seen anyone die, and she cried for some time. But after all, he has been so tired lately, she thought; now perhaps he can rest—somewhere that I don't know about.

But Matt walked up and down the stone hall weeping mightily and shouting, "He's always been here! And now he's not!"

Then Lovis said, "Matt, you know that no one can always be there. We are born and we die—that's how it's always been. What are you complaining about?"

"But I miss him," shouted Matt. "I miss him so much it cuts my heart!"

"Would you like me to hold you for a bit?" asked Lovis.

"Yes, you might as well," cried Matt. "And you too, Ronia."

So he sat leaning first against Lovis and then against Ronia and wept out his grief for Noddle-Pete, who had been there all his life and was not there any more.

Next day they buried Noddle-Pete down by the river. The winter had come closer; now it was snowing for the first time, and soft, wet flakes fell on Noddle-Pete's coffin as Matt and his robbers bore it to its place. Noddle-Pete had carved the coffin himself in the days of his strength and had kept it at the back of the costume chamber all through the years.

"A robber may need his coffin when he least expects it," Noddle-Pete had said, and in the last few years he had expressed surprise that it was taking so long.

"But sooner or later it will come to pass," he had said.

Now it had come to pass.

The loss of Noddle-Pete lay heavily on the fort. Matt was glum all winter long, and the robbers were downcast too, since it was Matt's mood that meant either sorrow or gladness in Matt's Fort.

Ronia took refuge with Birk in the woods, where it was now winter, and when she was skiing down the slopes she forgot all her sorrows. But she was reminded of them as soon as she came home and saw Matt brooding in front of the fire.

"Comfort me, Ronia," he begged her. "Help me in my grief."

"Soon it will be spring again. You'll feel better then," said Ronia, but Matt did not agree.

"Noddle-Pete won't see spring," he said grimly, and Ronia could find no comfort for him there.

But winter passed and spring came, as it always did, whoever lived or died. Matt began to cheer up, as he did every spring, and he whistled and sang when he rode out to the Wolf's Neck at the head of his robbers.

Borka and his men were already waiting down below. Hurrah, now their robbers' life was going to begin again at last, after a long winter! That delighted them, born to the robbers' life as they were.

Their children were much wiser. They delighted in quite different things, such as the disappearance of the snow, so they could ride again, and in the thought of soon moving back to the Bear's Cave.

"I'm glad you never want to be a robber, Birk," said Ronia.

Birk laughed. "No, I've taken an oath on it, haven't I? But I do wonder what we're going to live on, you and I."

"I know," said Ronia. "We'll be miners—what do you say to that?"

And then she told Birk the story of Noddle-Pete's silver mine, the one the little gray dwarf had shown him long ago in gratitude for his life.

"There are silver nuggets there as big as cobblestones," Ronia said. "And who knows, it may not be just a fairy tale! Noddle-Pete swore it was true. We can ride up there one day and have a look. I know where it is."

"But there's no hurry," said Birk. "Just make sure you keep it secret! Otherwise all the robbers will be in a rush to pick up the silver!"

Ronia laughed. "You're as wise as Noddle-Pete. Robbers are as eager as buzzards—that's what he said—and that is why I mustn't tell anyone but you!"

"But for the time being we'll be all right without silver, sister mine," said Birk. "In the Bear's Cave we need different things."

Spring grew more springlike every day, and Ronia was beginning to worry about the day when she would have to tell Matt that she was planning to move to the Bear's Cave again. But Matt was an extraordinary man; you never knew what he might do next.

"My old cave is a fine place," he said. "There's no better place to live at this time of year—don't you think so, Lovis?"

Lovis was used to his abrupt switches and was not particularly surprised. "Off you go, child, if your father says so," she said. "But I'll miss you!"

"But you'll come home again in the autumn as you usually do," said Matt, just as if Ronia had been moving in and out of Matt's Fort for years.

"Yes, I'll do what I usually do," Ronia assured him, pleased and surprised that it had been so easy this time. She had been expecting tears and shouts, and there was Matt, looking just as happy as when he remembered his own childhood pleasures in the old pigsty.

"Oh, yes, when I was living in the Bear's Cave it could have been worse," he said. "And that cave is really mine, don't you forget it! I might come and visit you from time to time."

When Ronia told Birk, he replied grandly, "He's welcome to come as far as I'm concerned. But," he added, "it will be a relief not to have to see that black curly head of his every day!"

It is early morning. As beautiful as the first morning of the world! The new inhabitants of the Bear's Cave come strolling through their woods, and all about them lies the splendor of springtime. Every tree, every stretch of water, and every green thicket is alive. There is twittering and rushing and buzzing and singing and murmuring. The fresh, wild song of spring can be heard everywhere.

And they come to their cave, their home in the wilderness. And everything is as before, safe and familiar. The river rushing down below, the woods in the morning light—everything is the same as ever. Spring is new, but it is still the same as ever.

"Don't be scared, Birk," says Ronia. "My spring yell is just coming!"

And she yells, shrill as a bird, a shout of joy that can be heard far away in the forest.